J

Lincolnshire
COUNTY COUNCIL
Working for a better future

discover libraries
This book should be returned on or before the due date.

To renew or order library books please telephone 01522 782010
or visit https://lincolnshirespydus.co.uk
You will require a Personal Identification Number
Ask any member of staff for this.
The above does not apply to Reader's Group Collection Stock.

EC. 199 (LIBS): RS/L5/19

Private Partners

GINA WILKINS

First published in Great Britain 2011
Large Print edition 2011
Harlequin Mills & Boon Limited,
Eton House, 18-24 Paradise Road,
Richmond, Surrey TW9 1SR

© Gina Wilkins 2010

ISBN: 978 0 263 22265 4

Printed and bound in Great Britain
by CPI Antony Rowe, Chippenham, Wiltshire

GINA WILKINS

is a bestselling and award-winning author who has written more than seventy books. She credits her successful career in romance to her long, happy marriage and her three extraordinary children.

A lifelong resident of central Arkansas, M. Wilkins sold her first book in 1987 and has been writing full-time since. She has appeared on the Waldenbooks, B. Dalton and *USA TODAY* bestseller lists. She is a three-time recipient of the Maggie Award for Excellence, sponsored by Georgia Romance Writers, and has won several awards from the reviewers of *RT Book Reviews*.

Thanks again to Kerry for all your help, and to Justin for patiently listening through a long Q and A session outside the tool stores!

Prologue

"Only one more week."

Anne Easton shook her head in response to Liam McCright's regretful murmur. "Don't say that. It makes me too sad. I can't enjoy our last few days together if you're going to be counting down the minutes."

They stood at a rock wall of the Argyle Battery of Edinburgh Castle, a breathtaking view of northern Edinburgh, Scotland, spread in front of them. Tourists with an intriguing mix of accents mingled around them, examining and exclaiming over the ancient cannons and battlements.

Anne and Liam ignored everyone else, concentrating exclusively on each other on this beautiful summer day.

A brisk, warm breeze caught her fine, blond hair and she reached up to brush a lock away from her mouth, but Liam's hand was already there. His fingertips glided across her cheek when he tucked the errant strand behind her ear, then bent his head to press a quick kiss against the lips he'd uncovered.

She smiled up at him, enchanted by the way his thick, dark hair, worn in his trademark long and tousled style, waved around a face so appealing that her throat still tightened when she looked at him. She couldn't see his blue-gray eyes behind his dark glasses, but she knew they were focused on her face as though nothing else around them was of interest to him. That heady attentiveness was one of his more seductive talents.

"I'll miss you," he said, pulling her into the crook of one arm to nestle her against his lean body as they turned to gaze out over the streets of the historic city.

"I'll miss you, too." The simple words weren't enough to express how much she would feel his absence in her life.

They had just spent a blissfully private eight weeks in London, and this jaunt to Scotland was a last celebration of their time together. In only one short week, she would return to Arkansas, where she would begin medical school in August, and Liam would fly to the Galápagos Islands on an assignment for his job as a globe-trotting journalist.

"I don't want our relationship to end this time. Not like the last time."

She bit her lower lip in response to the pain that shot through her. "There were reasons why we broke up three years ago. I'm not sure they've changed all that much."

"Except that you're an adult now, not an inexperienced college freshman. You're twenty-three years old, Annie. Your parents can't tell you how to run your life now. You have the right to be with me if you want, even if they still hate me."

"They don't hate you."

He snorted. "Right. Which is why you haven't even told them we've been together again for the past two months."

Because she wasn't sure she could win that argument, she said instead, "They weren't the only reason we broke up anyway."

"Maybe. But it's different now. The eight weeks that have passed since we ran into each other in London have been great, haven't they?"

"They've been perfect," she agreed wistfully.

As if on impulse, he turned to face her, using his body to block her from the view of any others around them, giving them a semblance of privacy in their very public surroundings. "Then why does it have to end?"

They both knew the answer to that question, but she shrugged and replied, "Because I'm starting medical school in Arkansas in just over a month and you're contracted to travel the globe

for the next year. Longer if your show gets renewed, which I know it will."

He brushed that logical argument aside with
characteristic impatience. "We don't have to be
joined at the hip to be committed to each other.
You can go to medical school and I can pursue
my career. We have phones and computers to
stay in touch when we aren't physically together,
and airplanes to get us both to the same place
at the same time whenever we have a few free
days."

She sighed, thinking of how unlikely it was
that such an arrangement could last the entire
four years she would be in medical school. Of
course, maybe Liam wasn't thinking that far
ahead. Maybe he was just thinking about playing it by ear after they went their own ways
next week. He wasn't known for long-term
planning.

"I would love to hear from you anytime you
want to call," she agreed. "There's certainly no
reason we can't stay in touch after we go back
to our separate careers."

He shook his head, his expression dissatisfied. "That's not what I meant. I don't want to be computer friends, or whatever the modern equivalent of pen pals might be. I want us to be connected. A real couple."

She laughed somewhat quizzically. "You want to go steady?"

"No." He wasn't smiling when he dropped his hands on her shoulders and gazed somberly down at her. "Marry me, Anne. Now. Before you go back to the States next week."

"M-marry?" Shocked into stuttering, she stared up at him. "Liam—"

He kissed her into silence, then raised his head with a new look of determination on his dashingly stubbled face. "Marry me," he repeated. "Let's make it official. Even if we aren't together all the time, no one can ever really separate us again."

Even as elation swept through her, she tried to keep herself grounded in reality. Liam had obviously lost his mind. He'd had a pint of Guinness at lunch—they both had—but she hadn't thought the ale was strong enough to addle his wits. "We can't just get married."

"Why not?" He grinned suddenly, letting himself get carried away with his reckless plan, as he was so prone to do. It was the trait that had landed him his coveted career. He was becoming increasingly famous as a daring adventurer who was willing to take great risks in pursuit of a marketable angle. "Who's going to stop us?"

"But—"

Glancing around at the new influx of tourists into their area, he took her arm. "Don't answer yet. Let's go have another pint and talk about it."

Shaking her head in bemusement, she allowed him to tow her away from the stone wall, though she promised herself she would not let him sweep her into an impulsive elopement. No matter how charming and persuasive Liam could be. There were entirely too many reasons why she couldn't go along with this crazy, impulsive proposal. Too many strikes against them from the start.

One of them had to be sensible—and that responsibility always seemed to fall on her shoulders.

Chapter One

"Are you sure you had the time to join us for dinner this evening, Anne? I hope we didn't disrupt your study plans."

"I can take off a couple hours for dinner, Mother. I can't study every minute of every day."

Though it felt sometimes as though that was exactly what she did, Anne Easton thought as she sliced into the roasted chicken her mother had served for this Friday evening family meal. Even when she tried to rebel and spend an afternoon resting or reading or watching TV, guilt and anxiety soon had her back at her books, working even harder than usual to make up for the lost time. Just as she would do tonight after returning to her apartment from this evening with her family.

"You've lost weight." Her mother, Deloris Easton, a retired family court judge, studied her intently from across the table. "And you look tired. Are you getting enough sleep?"

Anne couldn't help but laugh a little at that. "No. But don't worry, I'm getting by."

Her father, Dr. Henry Easton, Jr., a prominent and still-practicing Little Rock, Arkansas, neurosurgeon, listened to the exchange from the head of the formal dining room table. His thin silver hair gleamed in the light from the crystal chandelier overhead. Behind the lenses of his silver-framed glasses, his dark blue eyes focused piercingly on his only daughter. "It's all well and good to join the family for dinner occasionally. We enjoy spending the time with you. But don't let yourself get behind. You know what I always say..."

"Yes, Dad. If I fall behind, I'll never catch up," she recited, stabbing a glazed carrot with a bit more force than necessary.

"Back when I was in medical school, I was lucky to have a sandwich and a three-hour nap most days." Seated at the other end of the table, Dr. Henry Easton, Sr., retired thoracic surgeon, dabbed at his silver mustache with the corner of a linen napkin.

Anne's older brother, Stephen, had once suggested that Granddad had grown the mustache when the last of his hair had fallen out years earlier, just to prove he could still grow hair if he wanted to. Both Anne and Stephen had inherited their mother's blond hair and light blue eyes rather than the sandy brown hair and darker blue eyes from their father's side of the family.

Stephen, a third-year surgical resident and almost five years Anne's elder at twenty-nine, exaggerated a shudder. "Remember when I had the flu the second semester of my first year of med school? It was all I could do not to fall behind, even though I was feverish and aching and coughing my lungs up."

Anne focused on her plate, though her rapidly tightening throat made it increasingly difficult to swallow.

"I never missed a day of school due to illness," Granddad boasted. "Not a day of work, either."

Since she doubted he'd never been sick a day in his life, Anne wondered how many germs he had shared with associates and patients. Wisely, she kept that irreverent question to herself.

"You're making time to study for Step 1?" her father asked, referring to the first part of the medical licensing exam. "I know it's only early February, but June will be here before you know it. You'll want to be ready."

"Yes, Dad." She'd actually have three chances to pass the exam, but she knew her family would be appalled if she didn't sail through on the first attempt. Failure was not an option for an Easton, not even the type that would only set her back a few weeks on her long-term schedule. "I've already started going through the prep books. Whenever I'm not studying for a class, I work on the sample Step 1 questions."

"Not much time left for a social life, huh?" her brother teased.

Neither of the older men looked amused by the quip.

"She'll have plenty of time for a social life after she finishes her career training," their dad said firmly.

Their grandfather nodded agreement. "Just be glad you got rid of that McCright boy in college. Can you imagine how much harder this would all be if you had to stayed involved with him?"

"If she'd gotten into medical school at all," her dad muttered.

That McCright boy. It was the way they always referred to Liam, even though he was almost seven years older than Anne. He'd done a hitch in the army before enrolling in the university where they'd met.

They still blamed him for the B she had

received in chemistry her freshman year. For an Easton, a B might as well have been an F. Had she not been involved with that McCright boy, she would have been able to focus on her schoolwork, they had proclaimed.

Anne took a sip of her iced tea, pleased her hand was steady as she lifted the glass to her lips. It was her right hand, and a pretty little diamond and sapphire ring glittered on her finger. She'd worn it home from her year studying abroad after her college graduation, telling everyone she'd bought it as a souvenir in London. She never took it off.

"I saw him on TV the other night when I was flipping channels to find a good movie to watch." Her mother shook her ash-blond head in disapproval. "He was filming in another one of those dangerous, unstable places he's always going to. That long, floppy hair looked like it hadn't been trimmed in months, and he had at least a week's worth of stubble on his face. He looked like a pirate. I don't know how any woman could handle being involved with such a restless adventurer. I believe he's one of those adrenaline addicts I've read about. Never really happy unless he's risking life and limb somewhere."

Reckless, impulsive, footloose. Terms her family had used to describe Liam when she'd dated him that year. He had been all of those things, of course, and more. Had it been despite those traits or because of them that she had fallen so desperately in love with him?

Her dad abruptly changed the subject, as he always did whenever her college romance came up. "How's your car performing, Anne? Is it still giving you problems? Don't know why you won't let me buy you a newer one."

"I like my car, Dad. And it's running fine since you had your mechanic work on it for me. I don't need you to buy me a new one." It was the same car he'd given her for a high school graduation present six and a half years earlier. She had always intended to buy her next car for herself. She had certainly inherited her share of the Easton pride.

"Humph." He looked both annoyed and pleased by her refusal. "You always have been stubborn about letting me help you."

She smiled at him. "You raised me to be independent and self-sufficient, remember?"

His eyes softened. "So I did. What was I thinking?"

"Isn't this nice? I'm so glad we could all be here this evening. It's the first time we've all been together since Christmas."

"Not quite all of us, Mother." Stephen glanced pointedly at the empty chair beside him.

"Oh, I know, and I wish Danielle could have been here, too. Tell her we missed her, will you?"

Danielle Carpenter, another surgical resident, was on call that evening and couldn't leave the hospital. She and Stephen had been engaged for a few months, though they were in no hurry to set a wedding date. They seemed quite content for now to live together in their downtown Little Rock loft and focus all their attention on their jobs. Her family approved heartily of Stephen's choice for a mate. They considered the ambitious, brilliant and attractive Danielle a fine addition to their overachieving clan.

Both Stephen and Danielle had admitted they weren't sure they wanted children, though they weren't ruling out having one child in the future. Of course, they would be extremely busy in their surgical careers, but that was what nannies were for, right?

Having been cared for by several nannies during her own childhood as the daughter of career-obsessed parents, Anne knew it was possible to hire daily child care and still remain active and involved in a child's life. Her mother and dad had certainly kept a close eye on her. Still did, for that matter.

She had no doubt Stephen and Danielle would be just as successful at parenting as they were at everything else.

Anne prepared to leave not long after finishing her dessert. As much as she loved her family, she was ready to get back to her own apartment. She'd thought an evening break would do her good, but she was more stressed now than she'd been when she'd arrived. Her family didn't try to detain her; all she had to do was mention that she needed to study and they practically shoved her out the door.

Leaving the men in the den to discuss Stephen's chances of becoming chief surgical resident—something Anne had no doubt he would achieve—her mother offered to walk her to the door. Anne waited patiently while her mother reached for her aluminum cane, which she used to steady herself as she moved carefully through the large house.

Though only fifty-nine, Deloris Easton had suffered a massive stroke nineteen months earlier. It had happened only a month before Anne started medical school, only a few days after she had returned from abroad. Anne had brought home a secret she hadn't been able to share with her family while her mother lay near death for several days, nor during the long, still ongoing period of recuperation. Her mother had made great strides since her stroke, but it still broke Anne's heart at times to see the formerly robust and fiercely independent woman looking so frail and vulnerable.

"There's something I want to give you before you go, Anne. I found it when I was cleaning out my jewelry armoire earlier, and I thought you'd like to have it. It belonged to my mother." Her voice was only a little slurred, though it had taken a great deal of effort and therapy to achieve that success. Resting one hand lightly on the cane handle, she reached with the other into the pocket of the melon-colored blazer she wore with a matching shell and camel slacks. From that blazer pocket, she withdrew a small, flat jewelry box.

Anne opened the box curiously. She studied the necklace inside with a lump in her throat. Small baguette diamonds surrounded a larger, round-cut diamond that caught the light from the foyer chandelier and reflected it cheerfully back at her. The pendant hung from a deceptively delicate-looking gold chain. "It's lovely,

Mother. I think I remember Grandma Henderson wearing this."

"It was one of her favorite pieces. My brother gave it to her not long before he died in Vietnam. I know you'll treasure it."

"Of course I will." Almost unbearably touched, Anne reached up to fasten the chain around her neck. She'd worn her long hair pinned up, so it didn't get in the way as she secured the clasp. The pendant nestled into the neckline of the crisp blue shirt she'd worn with black pants for this family dinner. "Thank you."

"It looks lovely on you." Her mother sighed lightly. "I still miss her, you know. Every day."

"I know you do." Anne's heart clenched at the memory of how close she had come to losing her own mother. "Thank you again for the necklace. I'll take very good care of it."

"I know what a difficult time you're having now. I remember from Stephen's experience that the second semester of the second year is one of the most challenging parts of medical school. Several of his friends suffered severe burnout during that time, and I suspect Stephen was more stressed than he allowed us to see. I just want you to know your father and I are so very proud of you."

Anne was immeasurably affected by her mother's words. Yet, why did she now feel even more pressured than she had before? "Thanks, Mother. I'll try to live up to your expectations."

Her mother laughed and reached up to kiss her cheek. "We'll always be proud of you, no matter what."

Anne left without responding to that sentiment. As sweet and as heartfelt as it had been, she was fully aware she could disappoint her parents all too easily.

Anxious to get back to her studies, she parked her aging compact in front of her West Little Rock apartment and hurried up the stairs. Her small, two-bedroom apartment was on the second floor of the two-story, outward-opening building. She was already thinking about what subject she would study first when she paused in front of the door to insert her key in the lock. She wondered how much her study group had accomplished that evening. Maybe she should have met with them instead of taking the night off to dine with her family.

If she fell behind, she would never catch up.

Liam had always accused her of requiring too much of herself, on top of the expectations of her family. He'd told her she couldn't hope to be perfect, that she didn't have to live up to anyone's expectations but her own—which were set much too high for an ordinary mortal. He'd never quite understood what it was like to be an Easton.

Less than half an hour after arriving at her apartment, she'd let down her hair and changed into comfortable clothes—a T-shirt and yoga pants with fuzzy socks. She booted up her computer in preparation of a few hours of studying before she crashed for the night. It was only 9:00 p.m., so she figured she had three or four solid study hours before her brain shut down.

She had just plopped down in her chair to get started when her doorbell rang.

She wasn't expecting visitors that evening, and certainly not at that hour. Approaching the door warily, she ran through a mental list of possibilities. Maybe it was Haley from her study group, bringing by some notes or study materials, though Haley usually called before dropping in. Could be one of her neighbors, though she didn't know any of them very well, since she was rarely home and usually locked in with her books when she was there. Her brother, maybe? Had she left something behind at her parents' house?

When she looked through the peephole in the door and saw the face on the other side, she realized she never would have guessed correctly. It actually took her a moment to recognize him.

Disengaging the locks, she threw open the door. "Liam!"

"Hello, Annie."

"What on earth are you doing here?" Had she

somehow conjured him with her earlier thoughts of him?

Perfectly fitting the description, "tall, dark and handsome," Liam gave her the kind of wickedly charming grin that could make an impressionable young woman do all kinds of crazy and irresponsible things.

"I wanted to see my wife," he said in that beautifully modulated voice that whispered in her dreams so many nights.

Glancing instinctively around the otherwise empty landing to make sure no one else was within hearing, she moved aside. "Don't just stand there. Come in."

He didn't hesitate to accept the invitation. He moved through the open doorway, scooping her into his arms and kicking the door closed behind him.

The kiss seemed to last for a very long time, and Anne would have been perfectly satisfied had it never ended. Only the eventual need for air brought them reluctantly to the surface.

Opening her eyes with a dazed blink, she realized she had practically climbed Liam like a tree. Her legs were wrapped around his lean hips, and his hands supported her beneath her bottom. Her arms had locked strangle-tight around his neck. The metal-framed glasses he rarely wore sat a little crookedly on his nose and there was a smudge on the right lens.

Liam seemed to have no complaints about any of the above. He smiled at her with a flash of white teeth, looking as though he wouldn't mind taking a bite of her as he nuzzled her cheek and nestled her more snugly against his notably aroused body. "Now, that's what I call a welcome."

Her cheeks warming—though not as hot as the temperature burning deep inside the core of her—she disentangled herself and stumbled an inch or so away from him. He let her go, making no effort to hide his reluctance to do so.

Anyone observing their reunion would find it hard to believe they had parted in a quarrel only a few months earlier, she realized with a hard swallow. But then, it had always been that way between them. When they were together, the explosive attraction between them had a way of making them forget the many reasons why they shouldn't be.

She pushed her hands through the fine blond hair that tumbled in loose curls to the middle of her back. "I wasn't expecting to see you tonight. Why didn't you call?"

"I've been trying for the past hour. You didn't answer your phone."

She clapped a hand to her mouth. "Oh. I turned off the ringer earlier. I guess I forgot to turn it back on."

She hadn't wanted to interrupt her family dinner, and she hadn't even thought of her phone since. She hadn't been expecting any calls.

"You cut your hair." She'd noticed immediately that his signature mop of almost shoulder-length dark curls was now tamed into a cut just a little longer than military length, but she'd been too distracted by his kiss to comment at first. He looked so different without all that hair. She'd once teased him that his hair was more famous than his face.

His usual rakish stubble was missing, as well. He was clean shaven, his sideburns trimmed to a conservative length. With his glasses replacing his usual contact lenses, the change was quite dramatic. She studied him curiously, trying to decide how she felt about this new look. She'd never seen Liam with short hair, or looking quite so…well, preppy. He looked good—but then, it would take a lot more than a haircut to mar Liam's good looks.

"Yeah." He shrugged, his smile endearingly sheepish. "I guess this is my attempt at going incognito. You'd be surprised how well it works. I haven't been recognized all day."

"That's not so surprising at all. It really makes you look different."

"In a bad way?"

Amused by his sudden and wholly uncharacteristic moment of insecurity, she shook her head. "You look great. As always."

"Thanks. So do you."

Suddenly a little nervous, she ran a hand self-consciously down her faded T-shirt, rather wishing she still wore the professional, tailored clothing that had given her an air of confidence when she'd faced her family. "I just put on a pot of coffee. It should be ready now. Would you like a cup?"

Liam glanced at his watch. "Coffee at this hour? Is it decaf?"

"No. I was planning to study for a few more hours. I figured it would wear off by the time I turned in."

"Of course," he murmured, just a hint of disapproval on his face. "I should have realized you'd be studying. Am I interrupting?"

He was, of course, but she shook her head. "I hadn't even gotten started yet. I had dinner with my family this evening, and I've only been home for a little while."

"Ah." He followed her into her tiny kitchen, which seemed even smaller when filled with him. "That explains why you looked so tense when you opened the door."

"I happened to have a very nice time with my family tonight," she retorted, feeling the diamond necklace still nestled beneath her T-shirt. "They were on their best behavior."

"Didn't pressure you at all about your grades or your résumé?" He looked skeptical.

"Well…not too much."

He nodded as if she had confirmed his suspicions. "Mmm-hmm. Did my name come up tonight?"

She took two mugs from a cabinet to avoid looking at him. "What makes you think your name would come up during my family dinner?"

"Because it so often does. I'm the dire warning they use to make sure you stay in line. I'm sure they remind you you'd never be doing so well in medical school if I were still around. After all, I caused you to get that B."

He was so precisely on target she almost wondered if he'd somehow bugged her mother's dining table. Pushing that fanciful thought aside, she said lightly, "My mother mentioned she saw you on TV last week. Dad changed the subject quickly enough."

"I'm sure he did."

Following her father's example, she moved quickly to a topic less contentious than her relationship with her family. "Have you eaten?"

"Yeah. I had dinner a couple hours ago."

"Would you like dessert? I have half a chocolate cake hidden in the pantry."

Her wording seemed to amuse him. "What did you do, hide it from yourself?"

"No." She laughed and shook her head. "I hid it from my friend, Ron. He's a fiend for chocolate. I wanted to save some for snacks this weekend, in case I don't find time for a grocery run for a few more days."

"Ron?" His tone was carefully neutral.

"He's in my study group. I've told you about them. There are five of us in all. We get together several times a week to study our lecture notes and slides."

"Oh yes, I remember. So this would be old, ugly, married Ron?"

She lifted an eyebrow. She wasn't asking him who he spent time with when he wasn't around—wasn't even sure she really wanted to know. "No. This would be young, cute, single Ron."

"Humph."

She wasn't quite sure how to interpret that sound, but she had no trouble deciphering the look in his eyes when he moved closer and placed his hands on her hips.

"Actually," he murmured, "I have something besides chocolate cake in mind for dessert."

Suddenly breathless, she rested her hands on his chest, feeling his heart beginning to pound beneath her palms. "Do you?"

"Mmm." He bent his head to give her earlobe a teasing nip. "All of a sudden, I'm ravenous."

As was she. She melted into his arms, parting her lips in invitation as he pressed his mouth to hers. His tongue plunged eagerly, tangling with hers in a dance of desire.

"Annie," he muttered, lifting his mouth a fraction of an inch. "I've missed you. I hated the way we left things between us before Christmas."

"So did I," she admitted, remembering their quarrel with a sharp pang. She'd returned to Arkansas convinced that their unlikely marriage was coming to an end, which had made it very difficult for her to enjoy the holidays. She knew her family had attributed her unseasonable somberness to worries about her studies, but it had been Liam who'd been on her mind when she'd torn the wrappings from her gifts.

They'd talked since, of course. Neither of them had mentioned that painful argument, though she suspected it had been on his mind as much as it had her own.

His hands slipped beneath her top to explore the sensitive skin beneath. Ripples of pleasure seemed to trail from his fingertips as he caressed her throat, her breasts, her stomach—then lower. She moaned when her knees gave way.

Liam held her closer, and there was no mistaking he was as aroused as she. "Can you take

just a little more time away from your books?"
he asked, his voice hoarse.

At that moment, she would have gladly thrown
her books over a cliff. Whatever he was there to
tell her, whatever the future held for them, she
didn't want to waste one moment of their time
together.

Drawing his head to hers again, she murmured against his lips, "I'll start early in the
morning."

He swept her into his arms and headed back
toward the bedroom.

Anne lay against the pillows, waiting for her
heartbeat to return to normal—as if that were
possible with Liam sprawled in the bed beside
her. He lay on his back and his eyes were closed,
letting her see faint lines of weariness on his
handsome face. He'd probably had a long day
of traveling to get to her, though he hadn't let
exhaustion affect his vigor, she thought with a
sated smile.

She studied his profile, trying to get used to

his new appearance. Trying to convince herself he was really there. Wondering why he had come.

Her smile faded when she remembered the last words they had spoken to each other when they'd parted in December. Telling her friends and family she needed a little time to herself to rest and study, she had slipped away during her winter break to meet Liam in Memphis a week before Christmas. It had been only the third time they had managed to see each other in the past year and a half.

They had spent a long weekend at the famed Peabody Hotel, locking themselves in their suite and hardly coming out except for the occasional meal. It had been glorious, but had ended with an argument that had rapidly escalated into anger. The emotions between them had always been volatile and very close to the surface.

They had apologized later, but had parted rather stiffly, the words still ringing between them even as they had kissed goodbye. They'd talked only a couple of brief times since when

Liam had a chance to call from some distant place. Though they spoke cheerfully each time, she was often in tears after the calls ended. She hoped Liam didn't know that.

His right hand lay limply on his perspiration-sheened chest. Her attention was drawn to his ring finger, on which he sported a simple band of twisted gold and silver. She had presented the ring to him during their wedding ceremony, the same time he'd given her the diamond and sapphire ring she never removed. Every time she'd seen him on TV or in photos since, she'd noticed the band on his right ring finger, making her believe he wore it as faithfully as she did hers.

Tearing her gaze from Liam, she glanced beyond him to the clock on the nightstand. It was almost 11:00 p.m. With a smothered sigh, she slid toward the edge of the bed, trying not to jostle the mattress.

She hadn't realized Liam was awake until he spoke, his voice still huskier than usual. "Where are you going?"

She settled back against him. "I— No-where."

She didn't think he'd want to hear she'd been slipping from the bed to return to her studies. She could take another few minutes.

Opening his eyes, he turned on his side to face her, sliding a hand down her bare side from her shoulder to her hip. "You've lost weight."

"And you have a new scar since I saw you before Christmas," she commented, tracing a puckered line just beneath his rib cage on his left side. "Do I want to know how you got this?"

"Probably not."

She looked at his face. He looked utterly re-laxed, lazily content. His newly shorn dark hair was mussed into appealing spikes, showing hints of the curls he'd cut off. His clear, gray-blue eyes reflected his easy smile. Faint dimples creased his lean cheeks, bracketing the beau-tifully shaped mouth she so loved to kiss. She had always thought Liam was the most hand-some man she'd ever met. That opinion had not changed with the passing years.

Propped on his elbow, he toyed with the ends of her hair, pushing it away from her face and arranging it around her bare shoulder. "I guess we can agree that we both need to take better care of ourselves."

She conceded with a faint smile. "Probably."

"How's school going?" he asked, fully aware of the primary reason she hadn't been taking the best care of herself lately.

She shrugged. "It's pretty tough right now."

"How many subjects did you say you're taking this semester?"

"Seven. Microbiology, which includes immunology and parasitology. Pharmacology. Pathology. Ethics. Genetics. Behavioral science. And ICM—Introduction to Clinical Medicine 2."

He shook his head in consternation. "How do you keep up with all of that?"

"It's not easy. We have tests every two weeks, covering anywhere from fifty to eighty lectures per exam."

"Damn, Annie."

She could feel her throat tightening again. "I'll be studying all weekend to make up for taking the time off for dinner with my family tonight." Realizing what she'd just said, she blinked. "Um—how long were you planning to stay?"

His smile was just a little crooked. "Don't worry, babe. I won't interfere with your studying."

Wincing guiltily, she reached out to touch his face. "I don't want you to think I'm sorry you're here. It's always good to see you, Liam."

Dragging her hand to his lips, he brushed a kiss across her knuckles. "I've missed you."

"I've missed you, too," she admitted.

She had loved him almost from the moment she'd laid eyes on him more than five years earlier. She hadn't stopped during the years that had passed after they'd broken up so painfully during her freshman year in college. She'd only fallen harder when they'd met up again accidentally in London. Which probably explained how he had charmed her into this impulsive marriage that still seemed to have an unlikely chance of long-term survival—something she didn't want to think about just then.

He tangled one hand in her hair. "You didn't really want to leave just yet, did you?" he asked, his breath warm on her lips as he spoke only an inch or so away from her mouth.

"No. Not just yet." Wrapping a hand around the back of his head, her fingertips sliding into his short hair, she closed the short distance between them.

Studying could wait just a little longer.

Propped on one elbow, Liam watched Anne sleep. The bedroom was almost dark, but just enough light spilled in through the curtains and from the bathroom night-light to illuminate her pale face against the sage-green pillowcase. Her long, wavy, light blond hair tumbled around her in a rather decadent manner, falling across her bare shoulder and the upper curves of breasts visible above the sage sheet that covered the rest of her.

One strand of hair drooped over her left eye. He wanted to reach out and brush it away, but he was afraid of waking her. She needed her sleep. She looked exhausted, and he couldn't claim full credit.

Though he'd tried to hide it, he'd been startled by her appearance when he'd entered the apartment. It had been only six weeks since she'd sneaked away to join him for their weekend in Memphis during her Christmas break. He had commented then that he could see the toll her hectic schedule was taking on her, but the evidence was even more visible now.

She was too thin. Her light blue eyes were shadowed by purplish hollows her careful makeup didn't quite hide. She was still beautiful in his eyes; nothing could change that. But he worried about her.

He knew all too well the pressure her family placed on her. Almost as much as she placed on herself. That was most of the reason this marriage had been kept such a secret. Anne worried about her mother, who had been taken so ill very soon after they married. And she had said she couldn't handle the burden of her family's disapproval and disappointment on top of the stress of medical school. She needed her family's support and encouragement during the long stretches when she and Liam were separated, she had said. Though he tended to believe her family's support came with too many strings, he had agreed.

He'd had reasons of his own for going along with her request to keep their marriage to themselves. Yet he hadn't realized at the time how burdensome this sneaking around would become. Nor quite how much he would miss her when they were apart, even though he had known from the beginning that their time together would be limited.

Seeing how wan and tired she looked, combined with the sad condition of her pantry, had convinced him he'd done the right thing by coming here now. She needed him. She just didn't realize it yet.

He wondered a bit warily what she would say when he told her he had no immediate plans to leave.

Chapter Two

Liam wasn't in the bed when Anne woke Saturday morning. She lay very still for a few moments after glancing at the clock and noting it was just after eight. Her instincts told her she was alone in the apartment.

He wouldn't take off again without telling her goodbye. He'd probably gone out to pick up breakfast, considering there was no food in her kitchen.

She stumbled toward the shower, deliciously sore and loose-jointed after the night's activities. Running the water as hot as she could stand it, she scrubbed her skin until it glowed and washed her hair with a peach-scented shampoo she knew he liked. Rather than take the time to blow-dry the long waves, she pulled her hair back into a loose braid. She applied makeup carefully, accenting her eyes and brushing blusher over her cheeks in an attempt to look less pale and tired.

She'd just finished dressing in a bright green sweater and slim-fitting dark jeans when she heard Liam's key in the door.

He entered with his arms loaded with grocery bags. He hadn't just bought breakfast; it looked as though he had enough food to make a month's worth of meals.

She hurried to help him with the heavy bags. "You didn't have to do this."

"You said you have to study this weekend. When would you have gone for yourself?"

"I'd have managed. Eventually."

"Now you don't have to." Smiling over his shoulder, he moved toward the kitchen.

He wasn't wearing his contacts again this

morning. She'd always teased him about looking like Clark Kent when he wore his glasses. Deceptively mild-mannered and average. All it would take was a quick whip of his hand to remove both the glasses and the ordinary persona, turning him back into the daring, reckless superhero who had captured plenty of female hearts from the covers of travel magazines. He'd always laughed, but she could tell the comparison secretly pleased him.

They worked together to unload and put away the groceries he'd purchased. Now her pantry and fridge were better stocked than they had been in almost longer than she could remember. It amused her to think of Liam pushing a cart down the aisles of the grocery store, tossing items haphazardly into the cart. Still, his choices had been good ones, giving her plenty of options for quick, nutritious meals.

While they ate breakfast, he entertained her with stories about his most recent excursion to a politically unstable country in Africa, about some of the people he had met there, some of the adventures he'd had. She knew he didn't tell her everything; he was careful not to worry her about how dangerous his life could be, even though she was all too aware of the risks he took in pursuit of a story.

Liam had become moderately famous as a human interest reporter during the five years since they'd broken up in college. He was even the host of a weekly adventure-travel show on a popular cable channel, journeying all over the world to show settled-in-place couch potatoes what lay beyond their own familiar boundaries. The program had been renewed for another season, but as of the middle of December, he was on a three-month hiatus from filming during which he was concentrating on other work projects.

He was known as a daredevil and an adventurer, one who had the inside scoop on worldwide politics and cultures because he wasn't afraid to immerse himself in those foreign lands. She'd seen him eat fried scorpions in Beijing, ride a camel through the Gobi desert, dance with

Aborigines in Australia, tramp through South American rain forests and dive from a cliff in Hawaii. He'd accompanied African game wardens in their never-ending battles against wildlife poachers, interviewed extremists who would have killed him without hesitation if they'd thought they had anything to gain and covered a deadly raid on a Mexican drug cartel.

He'd been named by a popular gossip magazine as one of their most beautiful people, and was considered one of the country's most eligible bachelors. Refusing to answer questions about his personal life had only added to his mystique and popularity.

It had been suggested frequently that Liam led a charmed life. Anne couldn't help dreading the day when his luck ran out—another one of those things she tried not to think about too much. She was getting pretty good at sticking her head in the sand.

"You still haven't told me why you're here," she said as they cleared away the dishes after their meal.

"Yes, I did. I said I missed my wife."

She looked at him over her shoulder. "Now, how about telling me the whole truth?"

He laughed and shook his head. "I never could pull the wool over your eyes."

He leaned against the laminate countertop in the small, white-on-white kitchen, and she saw the glint of excitement in his eyes. Something big was up, she realized, slowly closing the dishwasher door. She braced herself.

"I have a book deal, Annie. That idea I pitched about a book of the stories I've been told by people I've met during my travels? I sold it."

Her eyes went wide. "Liam, that's wonderful!"

She stood and rounded the table to throw her arms around his neck. "Congratulations."

Returning the hug, he grinned. "The publisher is really enthused about the sample chapters I sent in. They like the angle I've given it—the way I interviewed senior members of so many different cultures and societies to get their take on world history as they saw it unfold. They think it's a sure bet to hit the nonfiction best-seller lists, and they think I'm a strong enough pitchman to make the publicity circuits and pitch both the book and my future projects."

She took his face between her hands and planted a kiss on his smiling mouth, her nose bumping his glasses. Laughing, he reached up to adjust them.

"I'm so proud of you. Why didn't you tell me sooner?"

"I had other things on my mind last night," he said, stroking a hand down her back and making her shiver in remembrance.

"This is so exciting. Is the book finished?"

"Mostly. I have to do some revisions. Quite a few, actually. First book mistakes, I guess. There will probably be more revisions to come."

"But still, they liked what they saw enough to buy it."

"Yeah." He looked a little dazed. "They did."

She kissed him again. "It's going to be a blockbuster. I just know it."

He'd already written several well-received magazine articles about his adventures during the past five years, but she knew he had always wanted to publish a book. She was thrilled for him that his dream was coming true. She was glad he'd told her in person rather than over the telephone.

She caught his hand as it sneaked under her top and placed it firmly back on her thigh. "So, what's the plan now? You'll hole up in your apartment in New York and work on your revisions until you start filming your show again?"

"Um." What might have been a nervous expression briefly crossed his face.

Her eyebrows rose as she sensed there was something he was hesitant to tell her. "What?"

"I can't get anything accomplished in my apartment. Everyone knows how to find me there. I thought if I crashed somewhere no one would ever expect, keep my head down for a few weeks, I'd get a lot more done."

"Where did you have in mind?" she asked, growing nervous herself now.

"I thought I could stay here. With you."

Her heart gave a hard thump in her chest.

"Think about it before you answer," he urged quickly, even as she slowly disentangled herself from his arms. "No one would have to know I'm here. You've said your parents never come here to you, that you always go to them when you want to see them. I can make myself scarce when you have your study group over, maybe go to a coffee shop or a library to work."

She laced her fingers together in her lap, her knuckles white from the pressure she exerted on them. "I would love to have you here, of course, but I'm so snowed under with classes and tests…"

"I could help you. Do the shopping, the errands, the housework, the laundry. You wouldn't have to worry about a thing around the house. That would free up even more time for studying, wouldn't it?"

She thought about her study friend Connor

Hayes, who had married during the past summer. Connor seemed somewhat less stressed now that he had Mia to share the load around his house, especially when it came to his seven-year-old daughter, Alexis. He was still as inundated with schoolwork as the rest of them, of course, but he'd confessed rather sheepishly that he liked having a wife to keep his household running smoothly. She remembered Haley had groaned and retorted that she wouldn't mind having a hunky guy to do all her chores while she concentrated on nothing but med school.

Now a hunky guy was volunteering to do that very thing for Anne. And she wasn't at all sure it would go as smoothly as he promised.

"I don't know, Liam. This has so much potential to blow up in our faces."

He leaned slightly toward her, sincerity etched on his handsome features. "We could try it for, say, a week or so. It shouldn't take me much longer than that to finish the revisions. If there's any hint during that time that I'm interfering with your studying, I'll clear out. You know I'd never do anything to cause you problems."

"Well—"

"Just consider it," he added with a smile that arrowed straight into her heart. "This could be the perfect time for us to be together. I don't have any other assignments for now, and you need some help around here. It would be the first time since we exchanged vows that we can actually live together like a normal married couple."

"A normal couple who have to keep their marriage a secret," she reminded him nervously, thinking of their quarrel at Christmas. Liam had been annoyed with her then for refusing to go to a popular Memphis nightspot with him. She'd declined for fear he would be recognized and too many questions would be asked, which had led to a heated argument about how committed she really was to their marriage. How much worse would it be if he had to hide in her apartment around the clock?

If he shared her memories, he kept his thoughts

well hidden when he nodded cooperatively. "That won't be a problem. I've left word I'm holing up to work and won't be available for a couple of weeks. No one's going to be looking for me, and I certainly won't draw attention to myself here."

The very thought of dealing with her family's shock and outrage if the truth came out, on top of her hectic class-and-tests schedule, made panic rise up from somewhere deep inside her that threatened to choke her. Her reaction must have been visible on her face, because Liam immediately reassured her again, "No one will know."

Though she felt a bit cowardly, she nodded. "That would be best."

He reached out to take her hands in his, his gaze holding hers captive as he spoke in a low voice. "I think we need this, Anne. You have to admit that we've been drifting apart the past few months. We need to do something about that."

Thinking of the tears she'd shed after their increasingly more uncomfortable phone calls, she swallowed painfully. Would Liam's visit repair the rift between them—or widen it? She was almost afraid to find out. And yet, she couldn't bring herself to ask him to leave. "I guess you're right."

He searched her face. "So I can stay?"

She moistened her dry lips. "We can try it. You said it would just be a couple of weeks?"

"Yeah, sure. Piece of cake to keep my presence quiet for that long, right?"

Uneasy with his too-optimistic attitude, she frowned. "I guess we'll see. But we'll have to be very careful. I just couldn't deal with my family right now if the truth got out. Not to mention the media attention you would probably draw if they found out you've been secretly married for a year and a half."

"I doubt I'm as much a celebrity as you seem to believe. With this haircut and my glasses and a baseball cap pulled low, I wasn't given a second look at the market this morning. But we'll be careful, anyway."

"Okay, then." She drew a deep breath, wondering if she were making an enormous mistake. "You're welcome to clear out a drawer and closet space for your things. You can use the small bedroom for your office. I set it up to serve that purpose for me, but I'm hardly ever in there. I usually spread out here on the kitchen table or on the couch in the living room when I'm not studying somewhere with my group."

"Are you supposed to meet your group today?"

She nodded. "We're meeting at one. We'll probably work five or six hours, but I can get away early if..."

"No," he interrupted firmly. "You won't change one minute of your schedule for my sake. If I see you only ten minutes a day, I'll be content with that. I promise you, Annie, you aren't going to regret agreeing to this plan. In fact, you're going to like it so much you're never going to want me to leave."

Which only gave her something else to worry about, she decided immediately.

"Will your neighbors be a problem? Do I need

to try to sneak in and out of your apartment while you're gone?"

She shook her head. "The apartment on the right, the one that shares my landing, has been empty for a few weeks. I think it's being re-painted or something. The neighbor on the left works nights and sleeps days, so I almost never see him. He wouldn't notice if a whole family moved in with me, as long as we're relatively quiet while he's sleeping."

"I'll keep that in mind." He moved toward the doorway. "I'm going down to get the rest of my things out of my car. Then I'll find a place for everything so my stuff won't be in your way."

"I can help you."

"Nope. I can handle it. You study or whatever you need to do this morning."

Hoping she would be able to concentrate with him moving around in the background, she nodded. They might as well get started on finding out if this impulsive scheme of his would work.

She wasn't at all sure she wouldn't have to ask him to leave eventually. The thought of doing so filled her with both dread and sadness that she pushed aside as she spread her books and her computer on the kitchen table.

Liam had seen Anne study before. Even on the few long weekends when she'd sneaked away to join him somewhere, she'd brought along her computer and notes. She'd always kept her books open and accessible even when she'd focused on him.

She'd studied at least a couple of hours a day when she was with him, and he had never complained, since he'd usually had responsibilities of his own to tend to. Both of them were much too busy to let an entire two or three days pass without at least part of that time being spent on their careers.

He needn't have worried too much about disturbing her, he thought with a wry smile. Sitting at the table with her computer and her books and notes, she didn't even seem to notice when he moved around in the kitchen at noon making lunches for them both. He set a plate holding a sandwich and a handful of raw baby carrots in front of her, and she blinked as if she'd forgotten he was even there.

"You need to eat before you leave to join your study group. This should hold you for a while."

"You really don't have to wait on me while you're here," she said, though she reached automatically for the sandwich. "I manage to feed myself on my own."

Not as often as she should, he thought with a glance at her slender frame. He decided he'd better keep that comment to himself. "It wasn't any trouble," he assured her. "It's just as easy to make two sandwiches as one."

When she'd eaten enough to satisfy him, she began to gather her books in preparation to leave for her study session with her group. "Did you get your things put away this morning?"

"I did. My clothes are in your closet and I set up my computer on the desk in the office and stashed my files in that empty desk drawer on the right side. Everything fit nicely."

"Good. You'll be able to work in the office?"

"Yeah, it's fine."

He didn't care for the politely formal tone of their conversation. This was one of the reasons he'd chosen to work here, from her apartment, for the next few weeks. If it was possible, he wanted to get back the intimacy they had shared that summer in Britain, before their separate career pursuits and her family had driven a wedge between them again.

"I'd better go," she said, picking up her stuffed backpack. "The gang is expecting me at one."

Even knowing she would be spending the next few hours studying with her friends, he still envied them the time with her. And even though she'd assured him they were only friends, he wasn't too happy that the group included two single men. He knew better than to express that objection, of course.

At least he had the satisfaction of knowing she

was his wife, and that she took those vows seriously—even if those other men were unaware of her status. During the past months, he had come to the uncomfortable realization that his impetuous proposal in Scotland had at least in part been based on a streak of masculine possessiveness he hadn't realized had been such a part of him. He hadn't wanted to let Anne out of his sight again without making sure she would be thinking of him when she met all those interesting young doctors-in-training.

It wasn't a motivation he was proud of, and he certainly knew better than to mention that bit of insight to Anne. She would have his ego for dinner.

"How long do your study sessions usually last?" he asked, keeping his tone deliberately casual.

She shrugged. "Depends on what we need to accomplish and whether anyone has other plans. Most weekends, we usually study for three or four hours straight, take a break, then go another two or three hours. Sometimes more, as the tests get closer."

He couldn't help frowning. "Long hours."

"Yes, well, we've already established that. As I've told you, I'm surviving."

Maybe so, but he didn't like the toll it was taking on her. Still, she looked a bit better this afternoon, he decided, studying her surreptitiously. She appeared more rested than she had when he'd arrived. There was a bit more color in her face now, and he liked to think he'd played some part in putting it there.

She tried to deal with too much on her own; that was the problem. Easton pride and self-sufficiency kept her from asking for help, even when she needed it. So he figured he would have to help her without being asked. By the time he finished his revisions, he wanted to make sure she was healthy and relaxed, prepared for anything medical school could throw at her.

Unlike her family, he cared more about her happiness than her accomplishments.

"I hope you get a lot done today."

She nodded. "Thanks. Good luck with your revisions."

He moved out of her way when she walked toward the coat closet to grab a jacket. Despite the extra bedroom, her apartment was more efficiency than roomy. The kitchen was so small that Liam had bumped against her several times while they'd put away the dishes. She'd merely smiled when he'd apologized. He knew she wasn't accustomed to sharing her space, but she didn't seem to mind the close quarters. For now.

He predicted that as her next test approached, she would grow even more tense and distant. He could deal with that, he assured himself. Maybe he could even help her relax occasionally. He had a few tricks up his sleeve for just that purpose.

He smiled in anticipation.

The study group gathered at James Stillman's condo that afternoon, as they so often did. James was single, his condo was spacious and his housekeeper always left plenty of home-baked snacks for their enjoyment, so they liked meeting there. He seemed to enjoy playing host, though Anne often had trouble reading James.

One thing she knew about him, he came from money. Perhaps that was just one child of privilege recognizing a kindred soul. The other three of their study group came from middle-class and blue-collar backgrounds, not that such social distinctions meant much when it came to the grueling demands of medical school. However disparate their backgrounds had been, med school exams had a way of leveling the playing field, so to speak.

James welcomed her in when she rang the bell. Though it was only ten past one, she was the last to arrive.

Tall and slender, with black hair and dark eyes, James always brought the word "elegant" to Anne's mind. She considered him a study in contradictions. He moved with a somehow utterly masculine grace, interacted warmly with their group of friends while still holding a part of himself back and studied as hard as any of them though the material seemed to come to him almost without effort on his part. At twenty-seven, he was the second oldest in the group, Anne being the youngest. James had obtained a PhD in microbiology before entering medical school. He'd explained that he'd decided too late to attain an M.D. to combine the two degrees into one program.

Haley, Ron and Connor gathered around the big table where they always spread their computers, books and papers, holding cups of coffee and helping themselves to chocolate chip cookies from a china plate.

Haley spoke first. "Hi, Anne. We were beginning to wonder where you were. You're never late."

"Ten minutes isn't very late." Anne dropped her heavy computer-and-book bag onto "her" chair and moved toward the coffeemaker.

"For you it is." Haley Wright smiled from the chair where she always sat when they met here. Of medium height, the amber-eyed brunette was slender and long-legged, though some-what more curvy than Anne. Anne was aware that she, herself, had lost a bit too much weight recently, resulting in a more fragile and waif-like appearance than she would have liked, so she snagged a couple of cookies to go with her coffee.

Sandy-haired, blue-eyed Ron Gibson had a smear of chocolate on his full lower lip when he grinned at Anne. "How was the family dinner last night?"

She rolled her eyes. "It was very nice—though I endured at least three separate lectures about not falling behind, in addition to maybe half a dozen stories about how much harder medical school was for my grandfather, my dad and my brother."

Always the clown, Ron laughed. "It's like I keep saying. You're sticking much too close to the family tree. You should have joined the circus or something and then you couldn't be constantly compared to the other family physicians."

She didn't have to fake her grimace. "Yeah, that would have gone over real well with the Easton clan. Their daughter, the circus performer. I might as well have driven a stake through their hearts."

Haley looked at Anne over the screen of her laptop computer. "Despite what you say, spending the evening with your family must have been good for you. You look a little more relaxed today than you have lately."

"I guess you're right." Anne busied herself with her own computer to avoid any further reply.

Ron released a gusty sigh as he dragged a thick stack of papers in front of him. "Man, they loaded us up with slides this week. We'll never get through them all."

"Of course we will." Ever the optimist and the group cheerleader, Haley spoke firmly. "We just have to keep pushing ahead, a few at a time."

Ron retorted with typical facetiousness, "That's all we have to do, huh? Gee, I wish I'd known it would be so easy. I wouldn't have had to worry so much."

Haley started to snap back at him, but James interceded smoothly. "Where should we begin? The pharmacology or pathology slides?"

Even as she participated in the ensuing discussions, it bothered Anne that Haley and Ron seemed to be quarreling more lately. The stress got to all of them occasionally, but Haley and Ron seemed particularly inclined to take it out on each other.

She still remembered an embarrassing incident last year when she'd broken down in tears in front of her study mates. She'd been overwhelmed with schoolwork, her mother had suffered a setback in her recovery, she hadn't heard from Liam in weeks and she'd been seriously sleep deprived. All of which had contributed to a meltdown that humiliated her even now when she thought about it. Her friends had been very supportive, which made her feel even guiltier at times for not telling them about Liam. Especially Haley.

The five of them had drifted together during their first semester to study as a group, and they had become true friends since. Anne didn't know what she would have done without them. While lying had become a part of her life during the past year and a half, she thought it was even harder to lie to her study friends than it was to her own family. Which seemed so wrong until she reminded herself primly that it was her family's own fault the lies had been necessary.

They had been studying for two hours without a break when Ron groaned and tossed down his pen. "I've got to move around, guys. My neck's killing me."

"How about a quick game?" James motioned toward the large-screen TV in his living room. It was connected to a top-of-the-line gaming system—another reason why the guys liked studying at his place. He theorized that game breaks helped keep the blood flowing to the brain, which increased the efficiency of their study time. Haley and Anne thought that was blatant male rationalization, but they didn't begrudge the breaks and often joined the games.

"I'm not in the mood to play today, but you guys go ahead." Haley stood and bent sideways to loosen her stiff muscles. "I just need to move around a little, then I want to check my e-mail."

She stretched, lifting her arms high above her head and going up on tiptoes. The movement made her blue knit top rise to show an inch-and-a-half gap of creamy skin above the waistband of her jeans. Anne noticed Ron focusing on that exposed area for a moment.

She had always wondered if there was something more to the sparring between Haley and Ron than either would admit—maybe didn't even realize themselves. Or maybe they really did just get on each other's nerves, she thought, telling herself not to look for hidden romances everywhere just because of her own situation.

She couldn't help laughing when the guys moved eagerly into the living room. "Just like three first grade boys when the recess bell rings," she muttered.

Haley laughed as she punched a couple of keys on her computer. "Exactly. You and I need to do something fun soon. Why don't we take a couple of hours to go shopping next weekend? I'm getting pretty desperate for some decent pants to wear on ICM days, when we're supposed to look professional. I can't imagine why they don't consider our usual class wear of ratty jeans and sweatshirts to be professional enough."

Anne laughed at the joke, then groaned, "You're forgetting Margo."

Margo was another student in their class. Known derogatorily as a "gunner," she was always at the front of the room, making herself very visible to the professors, highly competitive with her classmates, arguing for every extra point on the tests and making sure everyone knew her scores were among the highest every time.

Margo would never be seen in the jeans and

sneakers most of her peers wore to lectures. Her hair and makeup were always perfect, her clothing tailored and perfectly pressed. She even wore heels. Every day.

How Margo kept up her appearance and still managed the same grueling study hours as everyone else was anyone's guess; Anne certainly couldn't do it. Most days, she barely managed to throw on casual clothes and slap a little makeup onto her too-pale face. Her hair was usually in a loose braid or ponytail or clipped back with a barrette. She dressed the part of a doctor-in-training for her Introduction to Clinical Medicine days, when she actually saw patients under highly supervised and very limited conditions, but more often she looked like what she was. A harried student.

"Margo." Haley scowled. "The woman isn't human."

Anne chuckled. "You could be right."

"So, what do you say? Shopping? Next Saturday? To celebrate the completion of one more test cycle before we have to start the next?"

Anne considered the suggestion. Liam would still be at her apartment next weekend. But keeping in mind their agreement that she would go about her schedule as if nothing in her life had changed, she nodded. "That sounds like fun."

"Great." Haley laughed wryly. "It's not as if we have anything better to do, since neither of us have a social life. I can't even remember my last date. Can you?"

"Mmm." Leaving that to be interpreted however, Anne shuffled papers to avoid saying more.

"Maybe we should go to a bar and try to pick up a couple of guys. Just for fun."

Anne winced at the suggestion. "I don't think I'd be interested in that right now. I don't have time for myself, much less anyone else."

"I didn't say we should go looking for soul mates." Haley rolled her eyes teasingly. "Just a couple of Mr. Right Nows to entertain us for a few hours."

"That would require way too much energy. I'd rather just shop and then crash for a lazy evening before starting the next cycle."

"Like you're going to spend a whole evening not studying," Haley accused.

Anne laughed shortly. "You're probably right. But maybe I'll take a couple hours to soak in the tub and then relax in front of the TV or something before I start."

Both preferably with Liam, she thought, looking down at her books to hide any hint of that thought from her friend.

"Did you hear about Kevin Brownlee and his wife? They're getting a divorce. Laura told me yesterday."

"Ouch. That makes like the third divorce in our class this year, doesn't it?"

"We all knew how tough this would be going in," Haley said with a shrug. "How little time would be left to devote to anyone else. The spouses should have known, as well. Maybe it really is best to wait until after med school to even consider marriage. Personally, I can't imagine trying to juggle everything I'm dealing with now in addition to trying to keep a marriage together."

Anne swallowed hard. "I guess it would be easier if the spouse in question had an equally demanding schedule. A busy life of his or her own."

"So they would basically never see each other?" Haley frowned in consideration before shaking her head again. "Don't see how that's much better. Sounds like a setup for disaster to me. Growing apart, infidelity, that sort of thing. That's what happened to Vivien, you know. Her husband found someone to entertain him while she was studying."

Anne couldn't take much more of this conversation. "We're gossiping like a couple of my mom's friends at a day spa," she said with a light laugh. "We shouldn't."

"True. I guess I just have to remind myself sometimes why it's better that I don't have a social life. Why sleeping alone is the best option for the foreseeable future...even if it does get a little lonely sometimes. I can't even get a dog or a cat to keep me company. I'd feel too guilty about how little time I could spend with it."

Thinking about Liam sitting alone in her apartment less than twenty-four hours after he'd arrived to see her, Anne pressed a hand to her clenched stomach. "Um, Haley..."

James returned to the table at that moment, smiling at them both as he played the host. "Is there anything I can get for either of you?"

"We'd better get back to work," Anne said, deciding the interruption had been well-timed. This wasn't the occasion to spill her secrets to her friend. "We still have to go through the pathology slides. And we haven't even started micro."

Returning in time to hear her, Ron groaned and looked over his shoulder. "Better grab another cookie for energy, Connor. Anne's got that slave-driver look on her face again."

With a laugh, Connor slid into his seat and Anne pushed her personal issues aside to concentrate again on her schoolwork.

Afternoon was fading into evening when a quiet beep from Anne's cell phone signaled an incoming text message. Looking away from a mnemonic drawing Connor had created to help them remember several terms they needed to know for pharmacology, she glanced at the phone screen.

Sry 2 interrupt. R U eating out?

No, she typed in response to Liam's query. Almost done.

Connor had just commented that he had to leave in about twenty minutes to join his family for dinner, and James had said he had plans for the evening. He didn't share what those plans were, but then they were used to not knowing exactly what James did when he wasn't with them.

I'll cook. Any pref?

Srprz me, she tapped back.

She could almost see the sexy smile he wore as he replied, Gladly.

She slipped the phone back into her pocket. "Sorry. What were you saying, Ron?"

He looked at her, one sandy brow lifted quizzically. "Making plans with your secret lov-ah?"

"Yes," she replied without missing a beat. "We've just arranged an intimate dinner followed by a night of blazing passion."

Ron grinned in response to what he took as a sarcastic retort. "Okay. Touché."

Haley laughed. "I tried to talk her into going with me to a singles' bar to raise a little hell next weekend after the test, but she said she preferred staying home and studying. How boring is that?"

"I said I preferred a bubble bath and a couple of hours of TV," Anne corrected her, relieved her honesty had been rewarded—by everyone thinking she'd lied. "But I admitted I'd probably end up studying instead."

Ron's attention had turned to Haley, his expression uncharacteristically disapproving. "Were you serious? About taking Anne to a singles' bar?"

"We were teasing. But why not? Surely we

should be allowed some fun even in med school. We've got other classmates who make time to party between test cycles. Just because none of us particularly enjoy class keggers doesn't mean we can't let loose some other way every once in a while."

"At a singles' bar?"

Her smile growing tight, Haley shrugged. "It was just a joke, Ron. Let it go."

Connor started gathering his things. "We made a lot of progress today. I think I'll head on home to spend a little time with Alexis before she has to go to bed."

Giving Ron a now-look-what-you-did frown, Haley reached for her computer bag. "I'll finish looking through this stuff at home. Are we meeting tomorrow?"

"I have other plans for tomorrow." James set his notes aside.

"Maybe we should all study separately tomorrow and then get together after class Monday," Anne suggested.

Perhaps they'd been spending a bit too much

time as a group. Even the best of friends needed a break from each other occasionally.

Anne walked into her apartment soon after leaving James's place. "Hi, honey, I'm home," she called out teasingly, assuming Liam was in the kitchen.

He stepped out of the room she used as an office instead. Wearing a gray sweater that brought out the gray in his eyes, a pair of faded jeans and socks without shoes, he looked quite at home in her apartment. He carried a perfect red rose that he presented to her with a flourish.

Touched, she accepted the gift and lifted it to her nose, inhaling the sweet fragrance. "Thank you. Is this my surprise?"

"Oh, no." Snagging one arm around her waist, he drew her toward him, his head already ducking toward hers. "I've got quite a few of those in store yet."

Holding the rose in her right hand, she looped both arms loosely around his neck and brushed her lips against his. "I can't wait to see what they are."

His hands beneath her bottom, he hoisted her into the air. She laughed and locked her legs around his hips. "What about dinner?"

Carrying her as easily as if she weighed nothing at all, he moved toward the open door to the bedroom. "It'll keep another half hour or so. Let's start with something to whet our appetites, shall we?"

"I think that's a brilliant plan," she said, then pressed her lips against his again.

Chapter Three

"So, how did your study session go?" Liam asked when they settled in the living room a couple of hours after she'd returned home.

"Not bad. We got quite a lot accomplished, I think. What about you? Did you get started on your book today?"

He studiously examined his fingernails. "Um, yeah. Sort of."

"Not going so well?"

"I spent today sort of settling in. Setting up my stuff in the office, getting organized. I glanced over the revision letter again, but I thought I'd wait until tomorrow to really dive in."

"That makes sense. Do you have everything you need in the office?"

"Sure. All I really need is a place to set up my computer. The desk in there is fine. Comfy chair."

She smiled wryly. "Dad bought it for me. He said I need a comfortable place to study. I've sat in it maybe half a dozen times. I study a lot better sprawled on the couch or sitting on my feet in a kitchen chair than at a desk."

"Maybe that was the reason I couldn't concentrate in there. I'm not accustomed to being comfortable when I work. I've written most of this book in hole-in-the-wall hotel rooms, and on airplanes and buses, or wherever I could find a quiet spot to set up my laptop or pull out a pen and pad."

Her smiled felt a bit strained. "I guess you'll just have to get used to staying in one spot for more than a few days at a time, and having nothing to do except concentrate on your writing."

"I think I can manage that," he replied, his own smile bright. "Having you here—at least part of the time—is certainly a nice side benefit."

She wrinkled her nose. "I'm not sure how I feel about being called a 'side benefit.'"

He laughed. "No offense intended."

Settling against him on the couch, she leaned her head against his shoulder, enjoying the rare moment of intimacy. "I could probably take another hour off before I have to get back to my books tonight. Want to watch some TV or something?"

He rested his cheek against her hair. "I'd rather just sit here with you."

She liked the sound of that.

They spent that hour snuggling and talking and laughing. She could get used to this, she thought as they chuckled together over another funny story he told her about his travels. Too easily, actually. She had a difficult time returning to her studies when she could be nestled against Liam instead.

It was probably just as well he was only

staying for a couple of weeks. She could concentrate exclusively on her work again after he left. Assuming, of course, she didn't miss him too much to focus on anything but his absence, she thought uneasily.

She was up early Sunday morning, anxious to make up for lost time. While Liam had watched television, she had only managed a couple of hours studying last night. She'd assured him the noise wouldn't bother her while she sat at the kitchen table immersed in her books. She could study in noisy coffee shops, on buses and planes, anywhere she could find a place to sit with a book or her computer. She had the ability to tune out everything else except the material in front of her.

Although it wasn't always easy to tune out Liam. Several times last night she'd found herself gazing at him as he'd focused on the flickering screen, admiring the way the flashing light danced over his face, the way his mouth curved upward when he was intrigued or amused, the way he frowned when he disagreed with something spouted by a political "expert" on the news programs he favored. Each time, she'd had to force herself to return to her studies, though what she'd really wanted to do was climb into Liam's lap and taste that so-expressive mouth.

He hadn't said anything about how late she'd worked, though she'd become aware of his looks of concern and disapproval. She'd urged him to go on to bed whenever he got tired, but he'd assured her he was still adjusting to central time and wasn't ready to turn in yet. Finally deciding they both needed rest, she'd shut down her computer and accompanied him to the bedroom, where they'd fallen asleep wrapped in each other's arms.

It would be all too easy to grow accustomed to waking with him lying beside her, she mused as she turned on her computer for a new day of work.

Liam ambled out of the bedroom, his short, dark hair still wet from the shower, his face freshly shaven. His jeans looked old and comfortably worn, and the cuffs of his blue twill shirt were turned back to reveal strong, tanned forearms. He wore his glasses again, but the "mild-mannered reporter" image was negated by the slight swagger in his walk as he crossed the room, knowing she was watching him.

He stopped by the table to brush a kiss over her lips. "Have you had breakfast?"

She motioned toward the cup of coffee next to her computer. "I'm starting with caffeine. I'll work up to food eventually."

Shaking his head, he moved toward the refrigerator. "I'll make breakfast."

"That's not necessary."

"Oh, it definitely is necessary. I'm starving."

A common condition for him, she thought with a smile. Liam had the metabolism of a hummingbird, burning off calories even during the rare times he sat still.

She'd been so wrapped up in her studies that she hadn't even realized Liam had gone out to the newspaper stand in the parking lot until she saw the paper folded beside his plate. Trying to be a little more sociable than she'd been so far that morning, she asked, "Anything interesting in the news today?"

He shrugged. "The usual conflicts overseas, sniping between politicians and celebrity gossip. Lots of ink given to that ugly divorce between Cal Burlington and Michaela Pomfret."

Anne grimaced. She rarely glanced at Hollywood gossip, but even she had heard too many details about that famous acting couple's acrimonious split. It was particularly juicy because they'd made headlines only a few years earlier by leaving their former, equally famous spouses for each other during the making of a film in which they had costarred. Now there was a child involved, along with very public accusations of infidelity, emotional cruelty and substance abuse. "You've met Cal Burlington, haven't you?"

Liam nodded. "He was one of the three celebrities who appeared on that documentary I was involved with last year—the one about the crisis of the rain forests in Central America. The producers thought we'd get more viewers and attention if some big-name guests tramped through the forests with us to show the devastation there, though I lobbied for more screen time to be given to credible experts. Cal and I spent only a few days together. He seemed like a decent enough guy, despite the overinflated ego most actors have to develop just to survive in Hollywood."

"It must be humiliating for them both to have so much attention directed toward their private lives now. The painful breakup of a family shouldn't be fodder for public entertainment."

"No. But I guess it should be expected when they've spent the past decade doing everything they could to stay in that spotlight. They certainly weren't shy about exploiting their courtship and the birth of their child. Now they want privacy—and while I understand, and I believe they should have it while they sort out their personal problems, I can't help wondering if they're enjoying the attention in some twisted way."

Anne shook her head, suppressing a shudder

at the thought of living in such a fishbowl. Liam wasn't nearly as famous as Cal and Michaela, of course, but he had been steadily building his public reputation. His agent and publicists had been busy during this break preparing for the launch of the new season of his cable program. The publication of his book would make him even more of a celebrity.

How long would they really be able to keep their secret? And how much attention would they attract when they made their announcement?

She swallowed hard, hoping she would be prepared for that scrutiny when the time arrived. Sometime in the future, she assured herself. When they were ready.

Either growing bored or uncomfortable with the topic of celebrity marriages—or rather, the end of one, Liam changed the subject. "What have you been studying this morning?"

She was just as eager to move to a new topic. "Shigella."

"That's a bacteria, isn't it?"

"Yes. It's a rod-shaped, gram-negative, non-spore-forming bacteria. There are four sero-groups of shigella. *S. dysenteriae, S. flexneri, S. boydii* and...um...oh, yeah, *S. sonnei. S. dysenteriae* is usually the cause of epidemics of dysentery in close quarters such as the refugee camps you've visited."

She had recited the facts without looking at her computer screen, tensing when she'd momentarily forgotten the name of the fourth serogroup.

"Wow. That's a lot to remember."

She nodded grimly. "We have to know how many serotypes are in each serogroup, the differences between each group, what diseases are caused by each, the symptoms of those diseases and the medicines used to fight them."

"I don't know how you remember it all."

"That's just one organism. There are four bacteria in this lecture alone. We have to know as much about all of them."

"Is there anything I can do to help? I'd be happy to quiz you."

She glanced at the stacks of papers she had yet to wade through, including several pages of practice test questions. "Don't you have to work on your revisions?"

He shrugged. "I can work when you're in class and with your study group. Really, I'd love to do something to help you. I'll probably stumble over the pronunciations of all that stuff, but I'm willing to give it a shot."

"Well…"

"Okay, then. Let's finish our breakfasts, then I'll clear away the dishes and make a fresh pot of coffee and we'll get at it. The studying, I mean," he added with a wicked smile that made her giggle.

Having him here wasn't going to be a problem at all, she thought, feeling the muscles in her shoulders relax. As long as they continued to avoid drawing attention to themselves, she added silently, with one more little ripple of nerves.

"Okay," Liam said an hour later, "tell me again how many serotypes are in each serogroup of shigella."

"Group A, *S. dysenteriae,* twelve serotypes. Group B, *S. flexneri,* six serotypes. Group C, *S. boydii,* sixteen serotypes. Group D, *S. sonnei,* one serotype."

"Try again on Group C, *S. boydii.* How many serotypes?"

He watched the muscles tighten around her mouth as she sensed that her previous answer had been incorrect. "Sixteen?" she repeated, less confidently this time.

He shook his head. "No, it's eighteen."

"Damn." She brought her fist down on the tabletop in frustration, the thump making her third cup of coffee slosh perilously close to the rim of the large cup. "I always get that wrong. Why can't I remember? Eighteen. It's eighteen serotypes of serogroup C."

"You're getting too tense. Just relax."

"Relax? I've got to remember all of this for next Friday's test." She made a choppy motion toward the thick stack of paper in front of her. "That doesn't even count the four days of lectures this coming week—at least 480 more slides—that will also be covered on the test. Since I have no idea what questions will be asked from each lecture, I have to learn everything, just in case, and I can't even remember how many serotypes are in freaking serogroup C of this one bacteria! How am I supposed to pass the exam when I don't even know that?"

Her voice grew a bit louder and shriller with each word. Liam stood and reached out to take her coffee cup. He set it on the counter out of her reach. "I think it's time to switch to decaf. Or herbal tea. How about a nice cup of chamomile?"

"Don't tell me what to drink." She buried her face in her hands and drew a deep, shuddering breath.

He kept his voice soothing when he returned to the table and glanced at the next practice question. "How can *S. sonnei* be differentiated from the other serogroups?"

Without lifting her face from her hands, she answered in a muffled voice, "By positive b-D-galactosidase and ornithine decarboxylase biochemical reactions."

"That's right. See, you know this material, Annie. One little slip doesn't mean you'll fail the test."

"It isn't just one little slip! It's one of the easiest things I should know. How can I remember everything else if I can't remember that?"

"Annie." His tone was a bit firmer now. "How many serotypes are in serogroup C of shigella?"

"Eighteen."

"Right. And serogroup B?"

"Six."

"You've got it, babe. You'll do fine."

She groaned into her palms.

Liam walked around the table and placed his hands on her shoulders, feeling the knotted tension there. He began to rub slowly against the taut muscles, pressing his thumbs into her skin until she gave another little moan, this one of pleasure. With satisfaction, he felt her shoulders relax beneath his ministrations.

"That feels good," she murmured, arching like a purring cat into his palms.

He pressed a little harder against one stubborn knot, eliciting a sound that was half aah, half ouch. "How often do you panic like that?"

Sighing ruefully, she admitted, "At least once a day."

"That can't be good for you."

"I'm dealing with it."

"I've been doing a little research on stress in medical students."

She looked over her shoulder with a lifted eyebrow. "You have? Since when?"

"I did some computer searches yesterday while you were with your study group. Burnout in the latter part of the second year is very common."

"I'm not burned out," she said immediately, defensively. "It's just difficult to get through all the material."

He didn't respond directly to her denial. "Medical students tend to be overachievers, you know. Most were top of their class in high school and college, and it's a shock for some to be among evenly matched classmates. Students who were accustomed to being ranked among the top ten percent or higher are suddenly faced with being in the middle of their class—or even lower. That's a serious blow to the ego."

"I'm still in the top ten percent of my class." Her defensiveness seemed to be increasing as he spoke.

"That's great. But you know the old joke. What do they call the student who graduates lowest in his medical school class? Doctor."

He could feel her muscles start to tighten again. "I have to stay high in my class rankings to get into the most competitive surgical residencies."

"You haven't even started rotations yet. How do you know surgery is what you want to do?" He'd never thought she'd shown any real enthusiasm for that highly demanding specialty. He suspected her family of surgeons had heavily influenced her decision. "Maybe you'll like pediatrics. Or family practice. Or dermatology or psychiatry. Shouldn't you keep an open mind at this point?"

"I've always intended to be a surgeon. I'm considering neurosurgery," she added somewhat defiantly.

Which would add years to her training, he mused grimly. But wouldn't that impress Daddy?

He didn't point out that she said she'd always *intended* to be a surgeon. Not that she had always *wanted* to be. Maybe this wasn't the right time for this particular conversation.

Sensing his massage was no longer effective, Liam returned to his own seat and glanced down at the sheet of sample questions. "What are the two basic clinical presentations of shigellosis?"

Looking relieved the personal conversation was over, she seized on the question, answering with a renewed confidence. He wondered how much of that was feigned. It bothered him that she wouldn't allow herself to talk about her fears and doubts even with him. Her demanding, perfectionist family had really done a number on her, he thought with a slight shake of his head.

He had probably come as close as anyone to breaking through Anne's deeply ingrained Easton reserve. Yet he was aware there was still a part of herself she hadn't allowed even him to see. He wondered if he ever would—and if he would ever be completely satisfied with not having all of her.

Anne had been studying on her own for another three hours, after she'd convinced Liam to stop quizzing her and go concentrate on his own work, when her telephone interrupted her. Recognizing the ring tone she had assigned to her mother, she answered without glancing at the ID screen. "Hi, Mom."

"Hi, sweetie. I hope I'm not interrupting anything."

She pushed away the notebook in which she'd been scribbling key words for sequences she needed to remember. "I need a break, anyway. What's going on?"

"Nothing in particular. I just wanted to say hello."

"I'm glad you called. How was church this morning?"

"Very nice. Jenny Patterson was there. She said to tell you hello. Said she hasn't seen you in months."

"I should give her a call sometime. I'm afraid I've lost touch with a lot of my old friends."

"That's understandable. I told her you've been very busy. She said she understood. She's pregnant again. Did you know?"

"Again? Didn't she just have a baby?"

"Their little Anthony is a year old now. He'll be almost two when the next one comes along. Close together, of course, but Jenny said they planned it this way."

Several of her friends from high school were either expecting or already had children now, Anne mused. She couldn't imagine being responsible for a child yet. Nor could she envision a time in the next ten years or so when she would be in a position to become a mother.

"Annie, where do you—"

Holding the phone closer to her ear, she motioned frantically to Liam to be quiet when he entered the room talking. He grimaced when he saw the phone in her hand, and mouthed an apology, freezing rather humorously in midstep.

"Anne? Did I hear someone speak? Is your study group meeting there this afternoon? I'm sorry, I didn't mean to interrupt."

"You didn't interrupt anything, Mom. I told you, I was ready for a break." She didn't specifically lie about her study group, she told herself, though she was aware that choosing not to correct her mother's mistaken assumption was a deception in itself. "I always enjoy hearing from you. You know that."

"I'll let you get back to your studies."

"Okay. I'll talk to you later. Thanks for calling."

"I'm sorry," Liam said as soon as she set her

phone aside. "I didn't know you were on the phone."

"It's okay. That was my mom. She thinks you're one of my study group. I didn't bother to correct her."

"I did study with you earlier. So it wasn't entirely a lie."

She made a face at him. "Nice rationalization. Did you need something?"

"Oh. Yeah. Do you have any extra file folders lying around? I'm trying to get organized before I dive into the revisions."

She was beginning to wonder if there was a reason he kept procrastinating about those revisions. "There's a whole box of folders on the top shelf of the office closet. Far right corner. Help yourself."

"Thanks. And sorry again about the call. I'll be more careful in the future."

"Good idea. This situation is tricky enough."

"Don't worry, Annie. I promised I wouldn't blow our secret by staying here, and I'll keep my word."

"I know." She reached for her notes again. "Let me know if you have any trouble finding those folders."

"I will. Thanks."

Left alone with her books again, Anne gazed into the distance for a few moments before returning to work. Liam had seemed genuinely concerned he'd blundered into her chat with her mother. He'd always assured her he was no more anxious than she was to have their marriage discovered, by her family or by anyone else.

He'd admitted being seen as single was advantageous to his career. Producers were less hesitant to send him into potentially risky situations, celebrity magazines found him more intriguing and he didn't have to bother with answering questions about his wife or their unusual living arrangements. She had always secretly worried that he liked being thought of as single for other reasons, but she refused to dwell on those concerns now or at any other time.

They'd had vague plans to announce the marriage once Anne had a chance to prepare her family for the news. A month or two at the most, they'd agreed. They'd been prepared to spend most of their time apart for the first few years, but they hadn't really expected to keep the secret this long. Her mother's stroke had changed those plans. Anne just hadn't had the heart to upset the family even more at that time, and Liam had agreed—maybe a bit too quickly?—there was no need to go public anytime soon.

Just about the time when Anne had thought she couldn't maintain the lie any longer, her mother had suffered a setback. So, here they were, a year and a half into their marriage and still living a lie. It was no way to maintain a marriage, especially when combined with the long periods of separation. Their phone calls had been less frequent, their lives so different, so very separate.

She had tried to brace herself for the time when Liam confessed he had grown tired of the pretense—or worse, that he had met someone else. She had chided herself for not having more faith in him—in them—but the fears had lingered regardless. When she tried to look into the future, it was growing harder and harder to see them settled down together somewhere with the traditional picket fence and retirement plan.

Maybe this time together would reinvigorate their relationship. Or maybe it would show them once and for all they'd made an impetuous mistake on that beautiful summer day in Scotland.

The patient lay on the examination table in front of Anne and the other three medical students in her ICM group Monday morning, his thin body covered by a hospital gown, a tolerant smile on his lined face. He smiled at them all as they finished their lesson about his condition, Crohn's disease.

"Thank you, Mr. Dalrymple." She shook his hand, as did the other students, all thanking him for making himself available to them.

The patients they saw in ICM were volunteers.

During the first year, they had seen actors who taught the physical exams; this year, her patients had real ailments, giving the students a chance to see for themselves the physical characteristics of the maladies.

Anne thought she was getting pretty good at taking patient histories and doing a preliminary checkup, but she was still a little shaky with some of the more detailed exams. Second-year students spent so much time in class every day there was little chance for patient interaction. Her only real-world medical experience that year came from shadowing her preceptor, a surgical mentor who'd been assigned to her at the beginning of the school year, and whom she'd followed into the operating room three times since. She didn't actually get to do much during those days, but she was allowed to scrub in and observe closely. Dr. Burkhaven had even let her put in a few sutures the last time, which had been both scary and exciting.

She looked forward to third year. Step 1 would be behind her and she would rotate through several different medical specialties. She knew the hours would be long and her performance would be judged critically by the mentors in each area, but at least she would be seeing real patients, not sitting at a desk listening to seemingly endless lectures.

As they had agreed earlier, she met Haley in the cafeteria at just after noon. Both still wore their short white coats over professional clothing. The pockets of the hip-length student coats bulged with examination tools, note cards and pens.

Sitting at a small table with their salads, they had to raise their voices a bit to be heard over the noise in the large dining room. Employees and visitors milled around the room and sat at other tables, talking and laughing, some almost shouting into cell phones. Trays and silverware clattered on a conveyor belt that ran across the back of the room, moving dirty dishes into the kitchen for washing.

A pregnant woman sat at the table next to Anne and Haley, talking emotionally to an older woman who could be her mother. Anne tried not to eavesdrop, but it was hard not to overhear snippets of their conversation—apparently, the younger woman was experiencing difficulties and had been told she would have to undergo a C-section the following week, a bit earlier in the pregnancy than she or her doctors would have liked.

Anne would have liked to know what those complications were, but she refused to allow herself to blatantly listen in. She concentrated on her friend instead.

Haley had been telling her about the man she had met at a friend's house the evening before. "So, anyway, he seemed really nice and he asked if I'd like to go out for dinner sometime. I told him how crazy my schedule is right now, and he seemed very understanding about it. I said I'd think about it and let him know later today."

"Is he cute?" Anne asked with a grin.

"Very cute. Dark blond hair, blue eyes, a dimple in his chin that made me want to poke it with my pinkie finger."

Anne laughed. "So, have dinner with him. It could be fun."

Pushing a lock of brown hair out of her amber-brown eyes, Haley wrinkled her nose. "I'm tempted. But it's so hard to find any extra time right now."

"You can make time for a dinner with dimple-chin guy, especially this weekend, after the test."

"Maybe I will, then."

"You should. Remember what the counselors in the burnout prevention sessions keep saying. We should take breaks and try to live balanced lives—ha—or we'll suffer the consequences."

"Yeah, it's all I can do not to laugh out loud every time they make that speech. But I'll go to dinner with Dimples, anyway. That's about as balanced as I can manage right now."

"What's his real name?"

"Kris. With a *K*. His last name is Colton. I think. Anyway, I'll ask him if he wants to have dinner Saturday night. And then I'll put in an extra couple of hours studying Sunday to make up for it. Maybe I'll find something to wear when you and I go shopping Saturday morning. We're still on for that, right?"

"Sure. I can shop for a couple of hours. We'll find you something to wear that will knock this guy out of his shoes."

"What about you?" Haley looked across the table with a speculative look. "Want me to ask Kris if he has an available friend?"

Anne swallowed a bit of lettuce and reached for her water glass. "Um, no, that's not necessary."

"Are you sure? Like you said, it could be fun."

"I have plans for Saturday evening, actually."

"Family stuff, huh?"

"Yes." It wasn't a lie, she assured herself. Liam was family.

Haley pointed her fork like a disapproving fingertip in Anne's direction. "You need to do something fun yourself. And I'm not talking about listening to your dad and granddad and brother blow about their successful surgical careers. You need to let your hair down, find a good-looking guy, party a little."

Her thoughts going off in a direction that made her cheeks warm—not to mention other, less visible parts of her—Anne focused on her lunch. "I'll keep your advice in mind."

"You should."

Anne changed the subject. "You're joining us at Connor's house tonight, aren't you?"

"Oh, yeah, I'll be there. We're going to have to meet every night this week to get ready for the test Friday. This one's going to be a killer."

"They're all killers."

Her attention drifted to the next table again. The pregnant woman and her mother were standing, stacking their used dishes on their trays to carry to the conveyor. Anne glanced at the younger woman's bulging stomach, then at her face, automatically looking for clues as to her condition. High blood pressure? Preeclampsia? Complications of diabetes or some other disease? She saw no obvious signs, but then, she wasn't sure she would recognize the signs if they were present.

She looked forward especially to her ob-gyn rotation. Though she didn't plan to specialize in the field, she found it fascinating. The development of human life, the miracle of birth, the whole mechanism of the female reproductive organs had always intrigued her, though her father had always been somewhat dismissive of doctors who practiced in the field.

"Baby-catchers," he called them. Often women, these days. She didn't want to think that had anything to do with his attitude, but she didn't discount the possibility, either.

She was sure she would do well in a surgical career. She had the patience and the determination. She hoped she had the confidence. Surgeons were known for their self-confidence—to the point of arrogance, in many cases. She'd seen the lifestyle firsthand, so she knew what to expect. How little time she would have for a life outside the hospital. She could handle it. It wasn't as if Liam expected her to be a stay-at-home wife, any more than she expected him to be a stay-at-home husband. Assuming their challenged marriage lasted through the next ten years or so of her training, of course.

Because that thought depressed her, she glanced at her watch. "We'd better hurry. Class starts in ten minutes."

Haley heaved a sigh of resignation and gathered the remains of her meal. "Okay. I'm as ready as I'm going to be."

Anne returned home after classes to change into grubbier and more comfortable clothes for her study session. The group had agreed to meet at six-thirty at Connor's place.

Liam greeted her with a kiss. "How long before you have to leave again?"

"Just long enough to change and have a quick sandwich or something."

He nodded, and if he resented that she would be leaving again so soon, he kept it to himself.

He followed her into the bedroom, draping himself on the bed as she rummaged in the closet for jeans and a comfy, loose sweater. "Cold out today, wasn't it? I went out to pick up some supplies and that wind was bitter."

"It was cold. I'm ready for spring." She wondered where Liam would be come spring. In a desert somewhere? A jungle? The Antarctic?

He watched as she shrugged out of her white coat and placed it on a hanger in the closet.

"How was your day?"

"Long. The afternoon lectures were so dull, I nearly fell asleep. Dr. Emerson had ninety slides, with words so tiny we almost need magnifying glasses to see them. And he's the one who writes the nitpickiest questions for the exams."

"Bummer."

She smiled briefly. "That's one way to phrase it. How about you? Did you make much progress on your revisions today?"

He shrugged and made a sound that gave her no answer at all. Something about his expression made her suspect he'd accomplished little. She hoped he hadn't taken time away from his work just to shop and cook for her.

She reached for the top button of her blouse, then looked at him with lifted eyebrows. "Were you planning to watch me change?"

Moving with amazing swiftness, he came off the bed and stood in front of her, his hands covering hers. "Actually, I thought I'd help you."

Her knees weakened as the first button opened, revealing the curves of her breasts to his eager eyes. Liam had that look—the one that always ignited sparks inside her. She cleared her throat when he teased another button from its hole. "I don't have much time."

His grin was wicked. "Then we should make the most of the time you have."

Sliding her arms around his neck, she decided it would be worth missing dinner if it meant enjoying these stolen minutes with Liam.

Chapter Four

They were finishing the quick meal they'd thrown together when someone rang the door-bell just before six. Liam and Anne both froze, staring at each other wide-eyed across the table.

"Are you expecting anyone?" Anne asked in a low voice.

He frowned. "Of course not. No one even knows I'm here."

She scooted her chair back and hurried across the room, checking the peephole in her door. Her face paled.

Panic edged her stage whisper. "It's my father."

Muttering a curse, Liam grabbed his dishes and shoved them out of sight in the kitchen. Casting one quick glance at the table to make sure it looked as though she'd been dining alone, he almost ran into the office and closed the door behind him as the doorbell pealed demandingly again.

"Dad. This is a surprise." Anne's voice was a bit muffled, but still clear through the thin door of the office/bedroom.

Henry Easton, Jr.'s, booming voice was much more distinct. "What took you so long to answer the door?"

"I was, um, on the phone. Come in."

She wasn't a great liar, Liam thought, but her father was too self-absorbed to notice, anyway. He heard the front door close as Anne invited her father inside.

"Smells good. You cooked dinner?"

"I was in the mood for grilled ham and cheese tonight. I hope nothing's wrong at home?"

"No, nothing's wrong. I know you weren't expecting me. I guess I should have called first."

"You're always welcome here, Dad. Sit down. Can I get you anything?"

Liam glanced at his watch, hoping her father's surprise visit wouldn't last long. He could stay quiet, but he wasn't sure he hadn't left some clue to his presence lying around the apartment. The longer her father stayed, the more chance there was that he would notice something different.

"No, I can't stay. Can't even sit down. I've got a meeting to attend tonight. Just wanted to stop by and give you this."

Liam heard a crinkle—a paper bag, perhaps? And then Anne asked, "What is it?"

"It's a new Step 1 study guide. I ordered it for you a few days ago and it arrived today. I've heard good things about it. Wasn't sure you'd think to order it for yourself."

"Gosh, it's thick. Must have been expensive. Let me reimburse you for it."

"Not necessary. You know I want to do whatever I can to help you. Pay close attention to the pharmacology sections. And physiology, of course. A good deal of the Step 1 exam will come from those two sections, though you don't want to neglect any of the others."

"I know, Dad. We've talked about this. Thank you for the book. I'll start working through it the first chance I get."

"Good. Let me know if you have any questions."

"I will. Are you sure I can't get you anything? A cup of coffee?"

"No, I really have to go. Glad to see you're eating well. Your mother worries about your diet."

"She shouldn't. I'm taking care of myself."

"How are your classes going? Ready for the test this Friday?"

"I've been reviewing the material we've gotten so far. My study group is meeting this evening to go over today's lectures. We'll be meeting every evening this week to study the new material as we get it."

"Good. Glad you're keeping up."

"I am." Liam heard the door open. "Thanks again for the study guide, Dad. It was sweet of you to think of me, though you didn't have to order it. I would have done so for myself if you'd mentioned it to me."

"I can give my girl a gift occasionally, can't I?" her father asked with an indulgence that set Liam's teeth on edge.

He waited until he heard the murmured good-byes and the sound of the door closing before he risked peeking out to make sure Easton was gone. Anne stood in the center of the room, holding a heavy-looking paperback tome in both hands. The stress was back in her face, he saw immediately. The rosy color had faded from her cheeks, leaving her looking wan and drained. It annoyed him to see the results of even that brief of an encounter with her father.

"That," she said on a long exhale, "was close."

"You think we pulled it off? He really believes you were here alone?"

Tucking a strand of hair behind her ear, she

nodded in relief. "Oh, yes. He'd have said something if he'd noticed anything out of the ordinary."

"I thought you said your family never drops by unannounced."

"They don't, usually. That was the first time."

She still looked too tense, despite her confidence that they'd gotten away with their subterfuge. "You should finish your dinner."

She shook her head. "I've had enough. I'd better go join my study group. We have a lot of material to cover tonight."

She set the heavy study guide on the coffee table, looking down at it as if she were wondering how she would ever get through all of those pages in addition to the stacks of books, notes and guides already scattered through the apartment.

"Some gift," he grumbled. "He could have brought flowers or candy, but he brought more work for you to do instead. Real thoughtful of him."

He knew she'd taken the criticism wrong when

her chin lifted defensively. "Actually, it *was* a nice gesture. This guide probably cost close to a hundred dollars. And it should be very valuable in helping me study for the Step 1 exam."

"Why do you always make excuses for him, when all he does in return is pressure you into becoming what he wants you to be?" He honestly didn't understand her loyalty to her domineering father. How could she even pretend to appreciate the gesture when the stress of the drop-in visit was still evident in the lines around her mouth?

She looked away. "I'm not making excuses for him."

"Then why don't you tell him to butt out and let you worry about your own study schedule?"

"He only wants what's best for me, Liam."

"So do I," he returned evenly. "But you don't see me piling more work on to you and expecting you to thank me for it."

She sighed. "You just don't understand how it is between me and my family."

"No," he said flatly. "I guess I don't."

Liam's parents had split when Liam was young, and his alcoholic father had returned to his native Ireland not long afterward. Two years after that, Liam's mother died, leaving Liam to be raised by his mother's aging parents, now both gone. He'd been fond of his grandparents and had loosely reconnected with his father in the past five years, but he supposed it was true he'd never known the same kind of strong family ties Anne had with her family. Looking at the stress reflected in her eyes now, he figured he hadn't missed much.

He squeezed the back of his neck with one hand. "I don't want to fight with you about your father."

"I don't want to fight, either." Avoiding his eyes, she turned to clear away the remains of her abruptly interrupted dinner. "I'll just clear this stuff away and then I'd better go. You probably want to get back to your revisions, anyway."

"Yeah," he muttered, doubting he would accomplish much that evening. "I guess you're right."

* * *

The study group worked hard that evening, with even less small talk and foolishness than usual. Even Ron was uncharacteristically subdued and focused on the material. Anne had been warned by upper classmen that from February on, she would be inundated with material and tests, in addition to the rapidly approaching Step 1. One of her third-year acquaintances had particularly bemoaned the fate of Valentine's Day in the second year; the romantic holiday was pretty much buried between test cycles, which made taking the whole evening off from studying both perilous and guilt inducing.

Since Valentine's Day was over a week away, she had no idea if Liam would even still be with her by then. Even if he were, she would still have to devote at least part of the evening to her studies, which she was sure he would understand. They'd been half a world apart last Valentine's Day. Yet he'd still sent her a lovely card and a beautiful hand-dyed scarf from India.

But she couldn't think about Liam this evening,

she reminded herself for perhaps the dozenth time in the past couple of hours. She had to focus on the physiology, pathology and pharmacology notes.

"The three types of plague are bubonic, septicemic and pneumonic," Haley muttered, hands over her eyes as she committed the types to memory.

"Treatment for plague is antibiotics within the first twenty-four hours, ideally. First-line antibiotics are streptomycin or gentamicin," Ron recited, speaking to himself.

"And chloramphenicol for critically ill patients," Connor added.

James turned another page of his notes, silently internalizing the material. He glanced up to throw out a sample quiz question to the group. "Name two facultative anaerobes."

"Yersinia is a facultative anaerobe," Anne said, beating Haley to the punch. "As are Staphylococcus, E. coli and Listeria."

"Very good," James said with a smile. He

licked his forefinger and marked the air, as if awarding points on an imaginary scoreboard.

"Question for Haley," Connor tossed out, following their usual pattern of challenges and prompts. "Of Staphylococcus, E. coli, Corynebacterium and Listeria, which ones are gram positive and which gram negative?"

Haley groaned. "Wait, I know this. Only one is gram negative, right? E. coli?"

"Right. Twenty points to Haley."

Following a recent joking tradition, everyone made a writing motion in the air with their index fingers. It was the first moment of silliness in the past intense hour of studying. Anne could feel some of the tension among them ease as they sat back in their chairs grouped around Connor's dining table and stretched.

Judging it was a good time to interrupt, Connor's seven-year-old daughter, Alexis, a towheaded cutie with charming dimples and a gap-toothed smile, bounced up to the table. Dressed in pink pajamas decorated with gray kittens, she was obviously ready for bed. She was followed more sedately by her stepmother, Mia, an attractive woman with light brown hair and kind blue eyes.

"I'm going to bed now," Alexis announced to everyone as she paused by her father's chair. "Good night."

A chorus of smiling good-nights from the study group answered her. Connor gave her a hug and a smacking kiss. "Good night, princess. Sleep well."

"I will. Study good, Daddy."

He chuckled. "Yes, I will. Want me to come tuck you in? The group won't mind if we take a little break."

Alexis looked pleased by the offer. "Okay." Taking her father's hand when he stood, she waved again to the others. "Night."

James yawned. "I think I'll step outside for a minute to clear my head. Maybe the cold air will wake me up a little."

"Hang on, I'll come with you," Ron said, reaching for his jacket. "I need to go out to my car, anyway. I need the cord to my laptop. The battery's getting low."

"Alexis gets cuter every time I see her," Anne said to Mia as the three women sat around the table chatting while the men were away. "Is she really as well behaved as she always seems when we're here?"

"Pretty much," Mia replied with a pleased smile. "Connor or I rarely have to reprimand her, though it does happen occasionally. Usually for running in the house. She's always in such a hurry."

"Oh, to have that much energy again," Haley groaned.

"Seriously." Anne sighed wistfully before asking, "How's your school year going, Mia?"

Mia taught advanced English classes on a high school level. "It's been a pretty good year, so far. A few pain-in-the-patootie students, as usual, but that's to be expected."

"Are you still planning to start grad school next fall?"

"Yes. I've already submitted my applications

and talked to the admissions office. Connor and I figured we should be able to work around our schedules next year, since he'll have more evenings free from studying to help with Alexis. Connie Porterfield, the mother of Alexis's best friend, McKenzie, has already offered to provide after-school care and chauffeur services when both Connor and I are tied up."

"That was nice of her."

"She needs someone to watch McKenzie on weekends, when Connie works part-time. I figure I can study some while the girls play together on the weekends, and in the evenings after Alexis goes to bed. It will be a busy time for us, with Connor in his third year of med school and me in my first year of grad school and Alexis in the third grade at her school, but we should be able to work it all out."

Anne had watched Connor and Mia together, and they made a great team. Both were organized and goal-oriented, yet both put their family first even with all their other responsibilities. She didn't envision them being defeated by the obstacles that had already ended several of her classmates' relationships.

Whether she and Liam would be able to survive was another story...one she couldn't think about tonight.

Mia looked from Anne to Haley. "Poor Connor's been studying so many hours I can't help but worry about him, but at least he makes time to play with Alexis for a little while every day. That's good for both of them, I think. I hope you're both finding some time to just relax during this cycle."

Haley and Anne exchanged wry looks and shrugs. "We try," Haley murmured for them both.

"Speaking of which." Anne studied Haley over the rim over her coffee cup. "Did you ever call that guy? Kris with the dimple?"

"Kris with the dimple?" Mia repeated, looking intrigued as she studied Haley's suddenly pink cheeks.

"I sent him a text," Haley replied. "We're going out Saturday night."

"You have a date Saturday night?" Mia clapped her hands. "Good for you, Haley. You really deserve a break."

"Haley's got a date?" Connor rejoined them just in time to overhear. "Who's it with, Haley? Anyone we know?"

"It's no one you know. Just a guy."

"Who are we talking about?" James asked, slipping out of his leather jacket as he came back inside, his tanned cheeks a bit red from the cold night air. "What guy?"

Connor answered, "Haley's got a date Saturday."

"No kidding. Who with, Haley?"

Haley's cheeks were bright red now. Anne grimaced apologetically. She shouldn't have brought this subject up when the others could overhear, she realized. They would tease Haley mercilessly, just because they were guys.

Ron, she noted, had an odd edge to his voice when he asked, "Yeah, Haley. Who's the poor sap—I mean, who's the lucky guy?"

Haley shot Ron a scowl, then held up her

hands and shook her head. "It's no one any of you know, okay? And I'd like to keep it that way."

"How about you, Anne? Do you have a big date this weekend, too?" James asked, his dark eyes alight with his pleasant smile.

"I offered to fix her up, but she turned me down. Again." Haley shook her head in disapproval.

"I figure that's a good call, Anne," Ron gibed. "No telling what kind of clown Haley would dig up for you."

"Hey!"

Ever the peacemaker, James directed everyone's attention back to their purpose for being there. "We'd better get back to the books. Question for Ron— What's the first-line treatment for *Y. enterocolitica* infections?"

"Ampicillin or tetracycline," Ron shot back, his eyes still looking a bit dark as he slid into his chair.

"Fifty points," James conceded.

Everyone obligingly marked the air, but since

their light moods seemed to have evaporated, they went back to work without further foolishness.

It was rather late when Anne returned to her apartment, but Liam was still up. She found him in the office, slumped in the desk chair and glaring darkly at his computer screen. Several crumpled sheets of paper lay on the floor around him. They'd been ripped from the legal pad sitting by his right hand, as though he'd been making notes but had not been happy with what he'd written.

"How are the revisions going?" she asked when he turned in the chair to greet her.

She wasn't surprised when he sighed and answered, "Not well."

"What's the problem?"

He pushed a hand through his dark hair, then looked at that hand as if it still surprised him his hair was so short. Or maybe she was just projecting because it still startled *her* at times. "I'm not sure, exactly. I'm having trouble figuring

out how to handle the transitions between anec-
dotes. My editor said I need to make the segues
smoother."

"Maybe I can help. Would you like me to read
what you have so far?"

He smiled, shook his head and reached out to
turn off his computer. "You've got enough on
your plate already. I'll dive into it again tomorrow. I'm sure I'll figure it out. How did your
study session go?"

"We got through most of today's material."

Lifting an eyebrow, he glanced at his watch.
"It's after ten. It took you that long just to get
through one day's material?"

"I said most of it," she returned wryly. "I'm
going to spend another hour or two looking
over anything we might have missed."

"Don't you have an early class in the morning?
You should get some sleep."

"I will. After I've looked over these notes.
Feel free to turn in whenever you get tired. I'll
try not to disturb you when I come to bed."

"But, Annie, you need—"

She shot him a look that silenced him mid-sentence. "I need to study. I'll turn in when I'm finished."

Though disapproval was evident in his expression, he held up both hands in a gesture of surrender. "Fine. Do what you want. I'm going to watch some TV, then turn in."

She could tell he was a little annoyed with her for not listening to his advice, just as she was with him for trying to pressure her into doing so.

Arranging her study materials on the dining table, she bit her lip, wondering if she and Liam would even be able to survive a full week of living together. They had already quarreled twice today alone. That certainly didn't bode well for the state of their future marriage.

The noise of the vacuum cleaner Liam pushed across the bedroom carpet drowned out any other sounds in the apartment. He had only a couple of feet left to sweep and he'd be finished cleaning. The scents of lemon furniture polish and antiseptic cleaners filled the air, a fresh aroma that made him think of his grand-mother's Saturday-morning cleaning routine.

He'd scrubbed every surface in the kitchen and bathroom, mopped the kitchen and bathroom floors, dusted everything in the apartment and vacuumed every inch of the bland beige apart-ment-grade carpet in the living room and bed-room. It was almost four, and he'd been cleaning most of the day.

Running the vacuum cleaner over the last square of carpet, he flipped the switch to cut the power. The silence was immediate and quite a relief.

"Looks like you've been busy."

Turning, he saw Anne standing in the open bedroom doorway, her arms crossed over her chest as she leaned against the jamb and watched him.

Pushing his glasses up on his nose, he greeted her with a smile. Though she'd been in classes all day, after little sleep the night before, she still looked fresh and appealing in her crisp white blouse and dark jeans, her hair pulled back in a loose braid. He'd hoped to have time to freshen up before she came home. The gray T-shirt and faded jeans he wore with white socks were rumpled from his day's activities, and there was a smudge of grease on his shirt from when he'd cleaned the stove.

"I got restless sitting in front of the computer," he explained. "I thought a little physical labor would get my mind in gear. Besides, I know you don't have time for this sort of thing right now."

She kept her apartment tidy—mostly, she'd told him, because she didn't like coming home to a mess—but he knew it had been a few weeks since she'd had time to really scrub the place top to bottom. Now she'd been given a reprieve from trying to schedule that chore. It felt good to do something to ease her load at this stressful time.

She pushed away from the doorjamb. "How did you do on your writing today?"

He shrugged as he wrapped the power cord

around the hooks on the side of the vacuum cleaner. "I worked some this morning."

He supposed the nonanswer was an answer in itself. She could probably tell from his tone that he hadn't accomplished anything.

He had no idea why he was having so much trouble diving into this project. It wasn't like him to procrastinate when there was a job to be done. It was certainly out of character for him to be so full of doubt about his ability to competently complete the task. Lack of confidence wasn't really a problem for him; so what was this? He'd spent a lot of hours stewing about that today, and he still hadn't come up with an answer—nor accomplished any more on his revisions.

Seeming to sense his concerns, Anne asked, "Are you sure you don't want me to help you in some way? At least let me read the revision letter."

Liam waved a hand dismissively in the air. "I've got it covered. If I'm still having trouble with it in a couple of days, I'll call my editor and ask for some advice."

"But, Liam, I—"

Someone rang her doorbell three times in quick succession.

Anne and Liam froze.

"I'll stay in here," he said, waving at her to go answer the door. "I won't make a sound."

Nodding grimly, she turned and closed the door behind her. He hoped he wouldn't be trapped in here for long. He could really use a cold drink.

Silently, he sank to the side of the neatly made bed, making himself as comfortable as possible. This really was getting ridiculous, he thought a bit glumly.

He'd never expected to spend his marriage hiding behind doors.

Anne heard a child crying before she even reached her door. Puzzled, she looked through the peephole, then pulled the door open. She didn't know the young woman standing on her doorstep holding a screaming toddler, but she'd seen them before. The duo had moved into an apartment downstairs only a few weeks earlier. "May I help you with something?"

Speaking over the child's wailing, the woman—who couldn't be much more than twenty—asked a bit frantically, "You're a doctor, aren't you? I've seen you wearing your white coat with the stethoscope in your pocket."

"I'm a second-year medical student. What's wrong?"

Her dark eyes filled with tears, the slightly chubby brunette caught her child's flailing hand and held it toward Anne. "I'm Rose Duggar, and this is my son, Parker. He rubbed his hand over an old chest in my bedroom and he got a splinter under his fingernail. He says it really hurts. Can you look at it?"

"I'm sorry, but I really shouldn't. As I said, I'm not a doctor, just a medical student." For many reasons, primarily liability concerns, medical students were discouraged from practicing medicine without supervision. Anne was particularly reluctant to take that risk with a child she didn't even know. "Do you have a family doctor or clinic you can take him to?"

A fat tear escaped Rose's left eye, trickling pitifully down her pale cheek. "I just started a new job and my insurance coverage isn't effective until next week. I'm a single mom. I can't afford a medical bill."

The young woman looked as though she were going to sit on the step and wail with her child.

Anne sighed. She'd removed a few splinters in her time. Her friends in college had always come to her with their minor injuries because she'd been a premed major, her dad was a surgeon and she had a way of staying calm when others were freaking out. The latter reason had been more valid than the former two; she'd never quite convinced her friends that being a doctor's daughter did not make one qualified to practice medicine. Neither did being a second-year medical student, she thought, but she figured she could offer her assistance as a good neighbor, rather than a doctor.

"I'm Anne Easton," she said. "Please, come in, and we'll see if we can deal with this together. If it's only a splinter, it shouldn't be too serious."

"Thank you," Rose breathed, stepping quickly over the threshold with her son.

Parker screamed even louder when Anne tried to catch his little hand so she could see if there was anything she could do to help him.

She spoke in a soothing voice to him, "I'm just going to look at it, sweetie, okay? Will you let me see your hand?"

Only somewhat lulled by her tone, he drew a shuddering breath, fully prepared to shriek again at a moment's notice. His mother patted his back, her own expression heartened. "Let the doctor see your hand, okay, baby? Just let her look."

"I'm not a doctor," Anne muttered in despair. "I'm just a medical student."

The distinction seemed meaningless to Rose. She continued to gaze hopefully at Anne.

Vowing to herself that she would pay for the medical bill herself if the child needed emergency care, Anne carefully spread the little fingers and searched for the injury. She found it quickly enough. She was relieved to see that his mother had been right. It was just a splinter. It was a good-size sliver, but only partially buried in the tender skin. It would be easy enough to catch hold of the end with tweezers and pull the splinter out.

"Oh, it's not so bad. Why don't I get a pair of tweezers and then I can hold him while you pull it out," she suggested to Rose.

The younger woman's pale face bleached even more, with a slightly green cast to her cheeks. "I couldn't. I'd faint. I always faint with things like this."

"Okay, then you should sit down now." Alarmed by her lack of color, Anne ushered Rose to the couch, almost pushing her down to the cushions. If she was going to raise a little boy on her own, Rose was going to have to grow a thicker skin when it came to bumps and bruises and minor cuts—and splinters.

Making a sudden decision, Anne hurried to the bedroom door. Parker had started to cry again, not as loudly as before, but sounding tired and stressed. Probably he was picking up some of his mother's panic.

Anne opened the door and peeked in. "Could you help me out here, please?"

Looking a little surprised, Liam nodded and stood, moving quickly toward her. "What's the problem?"

She filled him in quickly, then turned to her neighbors. "Rose, this is my friend—"

"Lee," Liam cut in quickly, walking toward the couch. "Just call me Lee. And who is this fine-looking young man?"

"Parker," Rose replied shyly. "I'm sorry, I didn't know Dr. Easton had company."

"I'm not a doctor. I'm a medical student." Anne spoke a bit more forcefully this time, feeling compelled to make sure her neighbor understood that.

Liam knelt in front of Parker. "Hey, sport."

The toddler caught a sobbing breath, looking at Liam with wary interest.

"What's going on?"

"He has a splinter in his finger," his mother explained, her gaze flickering from Anne to Liam. "I'd take it out, myself, but I'm not good with blood. I thought maybe Dr. Easton would help me."

"Is it okay if I look?" Liam asked Parker even as he took the little hand in his own bigger paw. "Oh, that's not so bad. I could pull it out right now if my fingers weren't so big. Anne's not a doctor yet, but I'd bet she's got a pair of tweezers, don't you, Annie?"

"Of course. I'll be right back."

Leaving Liam to entertain the duo, she hurried into her bathroom for tweezers and an antibacterial ointment.

Chapter Five

Anne cleaned the tweezers thoroughly, then dipped them in a povidone-iodine solution to sterilize them. After scrubbing her hands, she carried the tweezers and ointment into the other room.

She was amazed to find both Rose and Parker smiling at some silliness Liam carried on with the child. It never ceased to amaze her how easily Liam could set people at ease, but she'd never seen him interact with a toddler before. He seemed to be pretty good at it.

At least Rose didn't appear to recognize Liam.

Maybe it was the difference in his appearance, with the short haircut and the glasses, or maybe she just didn't watch cable travel programming. Whatever the reason, Anne was relieved. She assumed Liam was, too, since he'd been careful to introduce himself with a shortened version of his name.

Parker looked as though he were going to cry again when Anne knelt in front of him with the tweezers, but Liam quickly distracted him by standing behind her and making funny faces. Rose watched Liam, too, rather than Anne— probably so she wouldn't get light-headed when Anne extracted the splinter.

Anne was pleased when the tiny sliver slid right out from beneath the little fingernail. She waited until Parker was in midlaugh at Liam's antics, and the child barely twitched when she quickly extracted the splinter. She cleaned his fingertip with an alcohol pad, dabbed on a bit of antiseptic ointment, then sat back in satisfaction. "There. All gone. Does that feel better, Parker?"

Parker looked at his finger, then held it up to show Liam. "All gone," he parroted.

"Why, yes, it is. Good job, Almost-Doctor Easton." He patted Anne's shoulder teasingly as she straightened. She gave him a look.

Rose stood, too, balancing her son on one rounded hip. "Thank you so much, Dr.—"

"Please call me Anne."

"Thank you, Anne. I don't know what I would have done if you hadn't been here. An emergency room visit would have been so expensive for such a minor thing, but I didn't want to leave it in there and let it get infected, and besides, it was hurting him."

"It was nothing, really," Anne assured her. "I'm sure you could have handled it yourself."

Rose drew a shaky breath. "I guess I would have tried, if you hadn't been home. I'm working on getting better at that sort of thing. My boyfriend used to take care of stuff like that, but we split up and he left town a couple of months ago. He's real good to send me child support money, so I can pay my rent, but it's still not easy being a single mom, you know? At least I've got real good child care for when I'm working. My aunt watches Parker for free because she's crazy about him."

It was a lot of personal information in one artless outburst. Anne merely blinked and nodded, wondering if Rose was always so forthcoming or if her image of Anne as a doctor made her so confiding. "I don't think Parker's finger will get infected. The splinter was in for such a short time and the whole area looks clean, but you might keep an eye on it for a day or two. Watch for pus or redness or swelling."

That wasn't medical advice, she assured herself—just common sense. It still made her nervous to treat a child without a license, even under these seemingly innocuous circumstances. At least she had Liam to verify that she'd made it very clear—repeatedly—that she was not a doctor.

"I have to go," Rose said, moving toward the door. "Parker and I are having dinner with my friend Vicky and her little boy, Jeremy. He's just six months older than Parker. We're having pizza. Parker loves pizza. I do, too, especially with extra cheese and pepperoni. Can I pay you for what you did for us, D—um, Anne? I can pay a little, just not as much as an emergency room visit would have cost."

"Absolutely not." Anne saw them to the door. "I enjoyed meeting you, Rose. And you, too, Parker," she added, tickling the little boy's chin and making him giggle.

"Thank you again. If there's ever anything I can do for you, please let me know. Nice to meet you, Lee."

"You, too, Rose. Bye-bye, Parker."

Parker waved his now splinter-free hand in Liam's direction. "Bye-bye."

Anne sagged against the door when she closed it behind her downstairs neighbor. "Whew," she said heartily. "That was an experience."

Liam laughed. "I'd say so. I was surprised when you called me out of the bedroom."

"I was afraid Rose was going to faint and the baby was going to keep screaming," she admitted. "I didn't think I could handle that by myself. Thanks for entertaining them both while I took care of the splinter."

"No problem. And no harm was done, since she hadn't a clue who I am."

He dropped into a chair. "Maybe you should suggest to Rose that she take some first aid classes. I mean, if she freaks out like that over a splinter, what's she going to do when Parker comes in with a busted head or a broken bone? Little boys are prone to that sort of thing, you know."

"So are little girls," Anne answered with a smile, fingering a thin, almost invisible scar beneath her chin. She had fallen off her bicycle when she was nine and then had run into her mother's immaculate house screeching and dripping blood.

Following her motion, he grinned and nodded. "Oh, yes, I remember you telling me about that. Children and accidents just seem to be connected, don't they?"

"I'm afraid so. If I see Rose again, maybe I

will suggest first aid classes. It's a good idea for anyone, especially a single mom."

"You'll be a great mom yourself someday," Liam said, his tone ultracasual. "You were very good with Parker. It's easy to tell you like kids. And you'll have your medical training to fall back on if they should get into a scrape."

She swallowed hard. This conversation reminded her of the recent talk with her mother about a pregnant friend and the direction her thoughts had taken afterward. She summarized those conclusions again for Liam. "It will be years yet before I'm in a position to even consider the possibility."

"Oh, I know. It's not like either of us is in a hurry, with you in school and me traveling the globe. But I don't know. Maybe someday?"

Keeping her eyes on her plate, she shrugged. "Sure. Someday. Maybe. Gosh, I'd better hurry. It's almost time to leave for my study session."

Liam let her get away with the change of subject. "I guess I'll work on my revisions this evening while you're gone. Maybe do a couple loads of laundry."

"You don't have to keep doing the housework," she chided.

He shrugged. "Gives me something to do while I'm sitting here, trying to be creative. I'm not used to being in one place for very long."

Which probably translated as he was already getting restless after being here less than a week, Anne thought glumly. She supposed she couldn't blame him. For a man accustomed to a frantic schedule, constant traveling and lots of interaction with other people, sitting alone in her apartment for hours had to be incredibly boring. The high point of his day had probably been making faces at a crying toddler.

Had he anticipated solitary confinement when he'd chosen to stay here?

The study group seemed to enjoy the tale of the splinter later that evening. Anne gave them all the amusing details, though she carefully left out any reference to Liam. All the others confirmed that they, too, had already been consulted for medical advice by friends and family who'd learned that they were medical students.

"They have no idea how little we've actually learned about dealing with patients," Haley groaned, looking at her stack of books and papers. "If they only knew that all we do is sit in class all day and try to memorize massive amounts of information that we'll probably never remember after the tests are over."

"I've been told we'll remember more than we anticipate," Connor commented. "I hope that's true."

"I just hope I can remember it all until the test Friday," Haley muttered.

"Then maybe we should get started," Ron said, opening a book with a thump.

Ron didn't seem to be in the best of moods that evening, Anne mused. His usual grin and bad jokes were notably absent, leaving him uncharacteristically grumpy. She supposed the pressure was even getting to him. Maybe he hadn't done as well on the last test as he'd hoped. Maybe he was worried about Step 1. Or maybe he had personal issues he hadn't shared with them. Whatever his problem, she figured that the best remedy was to dive into their notes and make sure they all did well on Friday.

"Question for James," she said, opening her binder. "What are the differences between granulomatous colitis, Crohn enteritis and Crohn enterocolitis?"

Anne stumbled into the apartment Friday afternoon so drained and exhausted after her test that Liam sent her straight to bed for a nap. He didn't have to twist her arm. She fell facedown on top of the bedspread and was sound asleep when he looked in less than ten minutes later.

He shook his head in disapproval. She'd had less than four hours sleep the night before. He'd talked her into going to bed at around eleven, telling her that she would do better on the test if she rested before taking it, but when he'd awakened at two, he found her side of the bed empty. She'd admitted that she'd woken up and hadn't been able to go back to sleep without studying for another hour or so.

She looked somewhat better when she walked into the office three hours later. Her hair was brushed and her face gleamed rosily as if she'd washed it to help her wake up. She'd changed her top, from the gray medical school sweatshirt she'd worn for the test to a more form-flattering dark red sweater. His heart gave a funny little kick at the sight of her, as it always did. Damn, but she was pretty.

"Are you working?" she asked.

He turned away from the computer. "Just answering some e-mail." He changed the subject before she could offer her assistance again. "Did you have a good nap?"

"I slept like a log," she admitted with a self-conscious smile. "I guess I was more tired than I even realized."

"No wonder. You haven't gotten nearly enough sleep this week. How did the test go?"

"Pretty well, I think. There were a couple of questions I wasn't sure about, but I think I knew

enough about the rest to at least make an edu-
cated guess at the answers."

"You must be glad it's behind you."

"I am. Of course, two weeks from today
we'll have another test. We'll be studying the
genitourinary system next. I'll start reading the
material this weekend."

"Fun."

She wrinkled her nose. "Oh, yeah."

"No study group tonight?"

"No, we're taking the weekend off. We'll all
study through the weekend, but on our own."

"Okay, then. Since you finished your last unit
and made it through the test, what do you say
we celebrate tonight?"

"Celebrate?" She looked intrigued. "How do
you mean?"

"Why don't we go out? Have dinner, see a
movie, maybe have drinks afterward. No one's
going to recognize me," he assured her, an-
ticipating her reservations. "I'll make sure of
that."

She looked tempted. When was the last time she'd been out for an evening of fun?

"Come on, Annie. It'll be great," he urged.

"Okay," she said in a rush. "Why not? As long as we're careful."

Delighted by her acceptance, he grinned. "Are you kidding? Careful is my middle name."

For some reason, she didn't look overly reassured by that quip.

She should have had more faith in Liam, Anne thought several hours later. As he had promised, he hadn't been recognized once during their evening out. They'd dined at a busy, somewhat dimly lighted restaurant, where their harried server didn't have time to study either of their faces. The food was good and they were seated at a comfortably private booth, where they were able to talk easily enough over the noisy background. Liam paid in cash rather than with a credit card imprinted with his name.

After dinner, they'd seen a movie they'd both enjoyed. It had been fun to snuggle in the dark theater, holding hands and laughing like an ordinary couple out on the town with nothing on their minds but each other. Now they sat in a cozy little bar in the popular River Market District, drinks in front of them as they watched the flow of people on the sidewalk outside the window beside their table. The glass wall could be pushed back in the summer, giving the illusion of an outside patio, but it was too cold for that on this winter evening. As much as she enjoyed the view, Anne appreciated being inside in the warmth.

A lot of young people seemed to be out on this chilly Friday evening, she mused. The bar was bustling, as were the other establishments down the street. Rock music played loudly from unseen speakers, combining with the noise of conversation and laughter to make a festive background as she and Liam sipped their drinks in companionable silence. They were both content for the moment to people watch and relax. Anne couldn't remember having this nice of an evening in quite a long while.

"I'm glad we did this," she said, setting her drink on the table and leaning forward so Liam could hear her over the din. "I've had fun."

He covered her hand with his and lifted it to his mouth, brushing his lips across her knuckles. "So have I."

"I'm surprised not one person has recognized you tonight," she admitted.

He chuckled wryly. "I suppose my ego should be bruised—but I can live with it as long as it allows me to spend an evening like this with you."

A couple of people had looked at him with slight frowns, as if trying to place him, but had shaken their heads and turned away rather quickly, apparently convincing themselves they were mistaken. Much to Anne's relief. "It's the glasses. And the hair. No one would have expected you to cut off all those curls. Have your agent and your producers seen you like this yet?"

"No. I had it cut only a couple hours before I caught the plane to Little Rock."

"Will they be upset with you? After all, your hair was so recognizable. So much a part of your image."

Frowning a little now, he shrugged. "I'd like to think what success I've enjoyed has been due to my work rather than my hair."

"I wasn't implying differently," she assured him quickly, her fingers tightening around his. "Like I said, it was just an image thing. Long, curly hair wouldn't have gotten you this far. Your talent and your personality have made you such a hit with your viewers."

Though his striking looks certainly hadn't hurt, she added silently.

Somewhat appeased, he murmured, "Thanks. The hair will grow back quickly enough, if I decide to let it. I haven't made up my mind yet."

"I like it either way," she assured him. "You'd look good to me if you were bald."

He grinned sheepishly. "I don't think I'll take a razor to it anytime soon. I have to admit, I whimpered like a little girl when the stylist made the first cut with her scissors. I'm getting used to it, but it still feels strange."

She laughed, delighted by his admission of vanity. She'd never made the mistake of thinking Liam was perfect, but the occasional reminder made her feel a little less daunted by the larger-than-life "image" she'd mentioned.

A commotion at a nearby table distracted them from their conversation. Turning her head to look, Anne saw a thirtysomething man frantically motioning toward his companion, a young woman sitting at a table with both hands at her throat, her eyes wide and her expression alarmed.

"She's choking!" the man said, looking around the room for help. "She's choking on a pretzel."

Anne started to rise. She sank back into her chair in relief when the woman grabbed a napkin, coughed into it and then coughed again, color returning to her face in a wave of embarrassed crimson. "I'm okay," she said, waving a shaky hand toward everyone who gaped at her. "I'm fine."

Her companion hovered over her, patting her shoulder and still looking a little frazzled, and a solicitous server approached them to offer assistance. The other patrons turned their attention back to their own business and the earlier lighthearted noise resumed.

Anne glanced at Liam. Rather than watching the other couple, he was studying her, a faint smile on his face. "You were ready to run to the rescue, weren't you?"

She made a face. "Knee-jerk reaction, I guess. I haven't learned much about treating actual patients so far in medical school, but I've known the Heimlich maneuver for years. You don't have to be a licensed physician to stop someone from choking."

"You'll be a good doctor, Anne."

She smiled at him. "Thank you."

"Anne?"

Her attention drawn again, she looked around in response to her name. "Oh. Nick. Hi."

Nick Paulsen was another member of her class. He and another man she didn't recognize had paused on their way to the exit when Nick recognized her.

Nick jerked his chin toward the couple that had caused the excitement. "Were you getting ready to run to the rescue?"

She laughed sheepishly. "Yes, I was. You?"

Nick's friend chuckled. "He was on his way. This guy can't wait to be a hero doctor."

"Stuff it, Grant. How'd you do on the test, Anne?"

She shrugged. "Won't know until we get the grades, of course, but I think I did okay. You?"

"Same here. Tough one, wasn't it?"

"Very."

"Okay, well, I'll see you in class Monday." He looked curiously at Liam, but Anne didn't bother with introductions.

"See you Monday, Nick. Enjoy your weekend."

"Yeah. You, too."

Anne looked at Liam again when the two men had moved on. "What?"

"He's got a thing for you."

She shook her head. "We're just friends. He asked me out last year, but I turned him down and we've moved on. He didn't hold a grudge— or a torch."

"You're wrong there. He's still interested. I know the signs."

Flustered, she picked up her drink again. "I think you're mistaken."

Though Liam was smiling faintly, his eyes were somber. "I just wish I could make it clear to him, and everyone else, that you're off the market."

It wasn't like him to sound so territorial. She wasn't sure how she felt about his tone. "I can handle that myself," she said lightly. "Let's talk about the movie. What did you think of the actor who played the big baddie?"

Liam hesitated only a moment before following her conversational lead. Perhaps he'd realized that this was neither the right time nor place to discuss their relationship.

As for herself, she planned to put off that conversation for as long as she could. Mostly because she had no idea what she would say if he ever asked her to choose between him and the vow of secrecy that she'd cravenly hidden behind for the past year and a half.

Chapter Six

In keeping with their agreement that Anne would continue with her schedule as if nothing had changed, she left Liam in the apartment the next morning while she joined Haley for the shopping excursion they had planned the week before. He assured her that he would utilize the time alone to work on his revisions and urged her to take as long as she wanted with her friend. She needed the girls' day out, he said.

Anne might have enjoyed the shopping outing a bit more if Haley hadn't had such a hard time finding anything that pleased her.

"What's the problem with this top?" Anne asked in bewilderment, motioning toward the very cute wrap-style blouse Haley was trying on. "It looks great on you. The color is very flattering."

Haley twisted in front of the mirror with a look of dissatisfaction on her face. "I don't know. It's pretty low-cut."

"No, it's fine. It's not too revealing, it's just flirty enough. You've got a great figure. What's wrong with showing it off a little?"

"I don't know…"

"Haley, this is the tenth top you've tried on, and you haven't been satisfied with any of them. That isn't like you. What's wrong?"

Haley sighed and shrugged. "I guess I'm having second thoughts about this date tonight. Maybe I should cancel."

"Why? I thought you said the guy's really nice."

"He is. I just don't really have time to deal with dating someone new right now. You know how it is."

"I know you need a night out to have fun." Anne thought of her own lovely time with Liam last night. "Trust me, you'll feel so much better after spending an evening away from the books."

"Oh, I know. It's just…well, first dates are so awkward and weird. I just don't know if I've got the energy for that now."

Which wasn't something Anne had had to worry about with Liam. After knowing each other so long, they were comfortable with each other. Most of the time, she mentally amended, thinking of the occasional awkward moment when they both tried to avoid talking about their future. Or her family. Or their unconventional marital arrangement.

Okay, maybe she did understand why Haley was hesitant to get involved with anyone now. Still, she didn't think one date would necessarily lead to the kind of complications she and Liam had gotten themselves into.

"Just go on the date," she urged, pushing her own quandaries aside to concentrate on her friend. "Have a great time. If you don't want to see him again after tonight, don't."

Haley smiled self-consciously. "You're right. I'm making a mountain out of a teacup, aren't I?"

"Confusing mixed metaphors notwithstanding—yes, you are."

It pleased her when Haley laughed before turning back to the mirror. "So, you really think this top looks good?"

"I really do. I'd tell you if I thought otherwise. Didn't I gag when you put on that pukey green one?"

"Yes, you did. I can always count on you to be honest with me, Anne."

Anne winced, but fortunately Haley didn't seem to notice.

Haley laughed and tossed the "pukey green" top over the door. "Hang that up for me, will you? I'm just going to try on this one last dress and then call it a day."

Anne had just hung the top on the rack provided for dressing room discards when the door opened again. She tilted her head with interest when Haley stepped out in a deep coral dress with a plunging scooped neckline and three-quarter-length sleeves. A soft, full skirt swirled beneath the belted waist, making the dress look very feminine, somewhat retro and quite figure flattering. "Oh, I like that."

"Do you?" Haley plucked at the stretched bodice. "I think it's a little too snug for me across the bust."

"Maybe a little. Do you want me to bring you the next size up?"

"No, that would be too big in the shoulders. It is a pretty dress, though. Why don't you try it on? Your boobs aren't as big as mine."

"Oh, gee, thanks."

Haley laughed. "Seriously, try it on. The color would be gorgeous on you."

Anne hesitated, then nodded. "Okay, sure. Not that I have anywhere to wear it, but it wouldn't hurt to try it on."

A few minutes later, Anne opened the dressing room door to model the dress for Haley. "It seems to fit pretty well."

"Are you kidding? It's perfect! See for yourself." Haley motioned toward the three-way mirror at the end of the short, dressing room hallway.

Anne eyed herself in the mirror. The dress did look nice. The cut emphasized her small waist, yet made the most of what few curves she had. The neckline was just low enough to hint at cleavage—not that she had any to show if it had been lower, she thought in self-deprecating humor. And the length of the sleeves made the garment pretty much a year-round style, very practical for someone living on a budget, as she was.

She thought Liam would like it. And that was all the impetus she needed to say impulsively, "I think I'll buy it. After all, it is marked down thirty percent."

"Always frugal," Haley teased. "You should definitely buy it. It has your name written all over it."

"I wouldn't go that far, but I do like it."

She stepped back into the cubicle to change into the clothes she'd worn shopping.

Haley spoke through the door. "You never said what you did last night. Did you crash at home, too, or did you do something interesting?"

Anne froze with one hand on the zipper of her jeans. "Uh—just a sec."

She finished dressing, ran a hand through her hair and picked up her purse and the coral dress before opening the door. "I went out for a little while with a friend last night," she said casually. "We saw that new action film that opened last week. The plot was kind of weak, but it was fun, anyway."

"Oh, yeah, I've heard it's pretty good. Who'd you say you went with?"

Haley's expression resembled that of a dog who'd picked up an interesting scent, Anne thought nervously. Maybe she hadn't sounded quite as nonchalant as she'd hoped when she'd mentioned her "friend."

"An old friend from college," she said, assuring herself it wasn't exactly a lie. "No big deal."

She must have done a better job of masking her emotions that time. When she immediately changed the subject to their class reading for Monday, Haley went along without further questions.

Driving the short distance home not long afterward, Anne entertained herself by making plans for letting Liam see her in her new dress. The next day was Valentine's Day. Most of the medical students had expressed pleasure that the informal holiday fell on a Sunday this year, rather than in the middle of the week when it would be harder for them to take time off from studying.

As for herself, she'd told Liam she wanted to celebrate the occasion with him at home in private, rather than braving the crowds in the local restaurants. After all, they'd just spent an evening out—and there was no need to press their luck on him not being recognized the next time.

She would study in the morning, then take off early to cook him a special Valentine's dinner—complete with candles and flowers and wine and a sinful dessert. It was definitely her turn to cook. She would change into the dress before sitting down at the table with him. A cozy, intimate evening for two, she thought with a smile of anticipation. Maybe she should have bought some sexy new lingerie to wear beneath the dress—not that Liam would notice. Once he had her out of her clothes, he rarely paused to admire whatever she'd worn underneath.

As a warm feeling spread deep inside her at the thought of how nice their private Valentine's Day celebration would be, she slid out of her car in her parking space, the new dress in its plastic covering draped over her arm.

"Hi, Dr.—er, Anne."

She smiled at Rose, who held little Parker's hand as they walked across the parking lot. Rose carried a couple of envelopes in her other hand, as if they'd just returned from a walk to the mailboxes built into a small, covered structure close to the apartment office

"Hello, Rose. Hi, Parker. How are you today?"

The toddler grinned at her. A smudge on his chin and a matching stain on his superhero sweatshirt suggested that he'd eaten chocolate recently. His cheeks were red from the exercise and from the brisk breeze that was beginning to blow stronger, bringing the colder temperatures that had been predicted for the next few days.

"I saw your friend Lee an hour or so ago," Rose commented. "He was just getting out of his car to go back up to your apartment. He's such a nice guy. He picked up Parker and tossed him in the air a few times. Parker loved the attention. He laughed and laughed."

"Lee's just a kid at heart himself," she said, the new nickname sounding odd to her ears. She wondered where Liam had been that morning. He hadn't mentioned plans to leave the apartment; she'd assumed he would be working all day.

"I could tell," Rose replied with a laugh. "He's so funny. Parker really likes him."

Murmuring something noncommittal, Anne made her escape and headed up the stairs to her apartment.

She found Liam sitting in the middle of her living room floor, surrounded by what appeared to be the parts to an assemble-it-yourself wooden bookcase. He frowned at the instruction sheet in his hand, his expression puzzled.

"Oh, hi," he said, glancing up from the paper when she walked in.

"What are you doing?"

"The shelves on the bookcase in your office are so overloaded they're starting to sag. I went out this morning and found one that will fit on the opposite wall. I think it will look good there—if I can ever translate these instructions into English," he added darkly. "Not sure what language this is, but it sure doesn't make much sense."

"I thought you were going to work on your book today."

He shrugged without looking at her and reached for a shelf. "I'll work on it while you're studying. Just wanted to take care of this first."

Shaking her head, Anne went into the bedroom to hang up her new dress, saying over her shoulder, "You really didn't have to do that. But it's a nice gesture, anyway."

"I'd hate to see your other bookcase collapse," he called after her. "The way you keep adding those thick medical books, it won't hold much more."

She couldn't help wondering if this was yet another excuse for Liam to procrastinate on his writing. Apparently he was having a hard time getting into that task. Granted, she'd never tried writing a book, but she couldn't figure out what was holding him back. It seemed as though it should be relatively simple; he'd already written a lot of it, now all he had to do was make the changes his editor had requested and finish the rest.

A short while later, she helped him carry the newly assembled bookcase into the office. As he'd said, the new case fit well on the opposite wall from her old one, and the style worked nicely with the room. She took a few books from the old case and arranged them on the new one, and she had to admit that it looked better not having her books so crowded together.

"I should probably start studying," she said, then waved a hand toward the desk that was almost buried beneath his notes and papers. "And now that you've taken care of my storage problem, you should start your own work. I don't like thinking that taking care of me is keeping you from the things you need to do."

Liam frowned. "I'm handling it."

She glanced at the overflowing wastebasket beneath the desk, the many scraps of paper on which he'd scribbled an idea, then crumpled and discarded. "Looks like you're having a little trouble. Are you sure there's nothing I can do to help?"

"I'm sure. Go study. I'll start working in here."

Though she wasn't entirely reassured by his tone, she nodded and left the room to make a fresh pot of coffee before diving into her material.

For the next three hours, Anne studied without a break, looking up only to refill her coffee cup. The material was new, and therefore confusing, and it didn't help that Liam couldn't seem to sit still in the other room. She heard him walking around, maybe looking out the window. Twice he came through to the kitchen, muttering an apology for disturbing her. Once he got a cup of coffee, the other time a soda and a handful of grapes.

She didn't think he got any work done. Resting her chin in her hand when a noise distracted her again, she glanced toward the office. He'd left the door open, and she could see him sitting at the desk. He had made a game out of tossing and catching the purple beanbag cat she kept on the corner of her desk. He was probably unaware that she could see him from her chair, and probably had no clue that his restlessness was affecting her studies. It didn't, usually.

A few minutes later, he wandered into the room again. "Can I get you anything? Something to drink? A snack?"

She glanced at her watch. "It will be dinnertime soon." And she'd gotten precious little accomplished.

"Oh, yeah. I guess you're right. I'll start dinner—what would you like?"

"You don't have to cook, Liam. We can order a pizza or something."

"If that's what you'd rather have."

"I'm just thinking about your time. I'm sure it's better used working than cooking."

His brows snapped together. "I know how to make use of my time."

Holding up both hands, she replied with a sigh, "Sorry. Just trying to help."

"Thanks, but it's not necessary."

His tone was still grumpy, which should have been a cue for her to back off. But because it bothered her that he seemed to be having so much trouble with his work, she couldn't resist offering a suggestion. "Maybe if you give yourself goals…you know, revise three pages before getting out of your chair, or try to do ten pages before calling it a day. That's the way I organize my study time."

"And I'm sure that's all very well for you, but it's not the way I work."

"Yes, but—"

"Look, I've got it covered, okay? Now, do you want pizza or should I cook something?"

"I'm not hungry," she said, deliberately opening a textbook.

"You should eat something."

Her response was curt. "I don't need you to tell me when to eat."

Their terse words seemed to hang in the air for a long minute. And then Liam shook his head. "This is no good. You're stressed, I'm stressed—but we shouldn't take it out on each other."

Still stinging from the tone he had taken with

her, she wanted to remind him childishly that he had started it—but he was right. Snarling at each other would not help either of them.

She nodded, but couldn't resist adding, "I was just trying to help. The way you've been helping me."

"I know, and I'm sorry. It's just not going very well, you know? I'm having a hell of a time figuring out what to do with this book. I'm beginning to wonder if I'm going to be able to do this, after all."

His uncharacteristic expression of self-doubt dampened her anger even more. "Of course you'll be able to do it, Liam. I have complete faith in you."

He sighed heavily. "Thanks, Annie. I'm sure you're right. I'll figure it out, eventually. It's just been more difficult than I anticipated. I'm really sorry I'm interfering with your studying. Maybe I should just—"

"Order a pizza," she finished for him quickly. "With mushrooms, black olives and green peppers."

Nodding, he turned toward the kitchen, leaving her to return to her studies until the pizza arrived.

Trying to focus on her notes, she chewed her lower lip. She knew what Liam had been about to say when she'd interrupted so hastily. He'd been on the verge of suggesting that he should leave, go back to New York, perhaps. And while it was probably true that she would study more easily without him here, when it came to having him say the words, she'd realized abruptly that she wasn't ready for him to go.

He would leave eventually, she reminded herself. He'd said from the day he'd arrived that he wouldn't be staying long. She had even been privately relieved to hear that at the time.

It was hard to keep his presence secret, hard to concentrate entirely on her studies while he was here and difficult for both of them to handle the stress of their careers without occasionally turning on each other. She supposed that was only normal for two people cooped up in such close quarters under such difficult circumstances.

But she still wasn't ready for him to leave. She wasn't sure she would ever be entirely ready for that, no matter how diligently she tried to prepare herself. And if they reached a point where she *did* want him to go—what would that say about the future of their relationship?

Anne was startled awake at three o'clock Sunday morning by the buzz of a cell phone. Groggy and disoriented, she started to fumble for her phone, then realized that Liam had already answered his own.

He said only a few words, then she heard him end the conversation with, "I'll be there as soon as I can."

She'd been asleep less than three hours, having turned in at just after midnight, when she'd been unable to study any longer. She pushed her hair out of her face to peer at him when he pushed back the covers and swung his legs over the edge of the bed. "Where are you going?"

"Sorry to wake you. That was my aunt Maura."

She frowned. "Your father's sister? The one in Ireland?"

"Yes. Dungarvan."

"Is something wrong with your dad?"

She heard Liam swallow before he said, "He's had a heart attack."

She pushed herself upright. "Oh, Liam—"

He held up a hand that looked reassuringly steady in the shadows. "Maura said they're cautiously optimistic about his recovery at this point, but she thought I would want to know. I think I should go there."

"Of course you should!" Climbing out of the bed, she turned on the lights, squinting a little until her eyes adjusted. She watched as he pulled his bags out of the closet. Thinking of everything she had to do during the next two weeks, she drew a deep breath and asked, "Do you want me to come with you?"

He stilled in the process of taking shirts from hangers. His eyes were soft when he looked at her. "I can't tell you how much it means to me that you offered—but, no. There's no need for that."

"You're sure? Because Haley could take notes for me."

He shook his head firmly, returning to his packing. "You keep up with your classes and I'll take care of my dad. I'll call, of course."

"Yes, please do. I'll be worried."

Forty-five minutes later, showered, shaved and dressed, Liam packed his bags in his car, then returned to make sure he had everything and to kiss Anne goodbye. "I'll call when I get there."

"All right. Have a safe trip."

He held her tightly for a long hug, then reluctantly let her go. "Try to get some more sleep. You need the rest."

With that, he let himself out, closing the door quietly behind him.

Her arms locked across her chest, Anne blinked back tears as she stared blindly at that closed door. She wasn't entirely sure Liam would return to Little Rock once he'd assured himself that his father no longer needed him. Especially after the silly quarrel they'd had before dinner. He would just as likely decide that he should go back to his own apartment in New York, that his little experiment of living with her had not worked out as he'd hoped.

It hadn't escaped her attention that he'd taken everything with him when he departed, leaving an emptiness inside her that felt much larger than the gap in her closet. Maybe he had privately realized he couldn't work here, after all. She was aware of just how little he'd accomplished during the past week, though he hadn't been willing to discuss his progress—or lack thereof.

Maybe he was tired of hiding behind doors whenever her doorbell rang. Or sitting alone in her apartment while she spent hours in classes and with her study group. She certainly couldn't blame him for that.

Wiping her damp cheeks with an impatient hand, she turned away from the door and moved toward the kitchen. She might as well make a pot of coffee. She couldn't sleep now, anyway.

She had just poured her first, fragrant cup when it occurred to her that this was Valentine's Day.

Swearing beneath her breath, she told herself it didn't matter. It was a silly, made-up holiday, anyway, and Liam had much more important things on his mind. They both did.

She carried the cup to the table, set it down with a thump and opened her laptop. She had to study; she didn't have time to stand there and sniffle.

But she really was going to miss him.

The phone rang at just after noon, drawing Anne out of her perusal of a drawing of the male reproductive system. She'd already been studying for almost eight hours, even though she hadn't even had lunch yet. She was getting tired after so little sleep, but she'd figured she might as well study another hour or so, then take a brief nap before diving in again.

She snatched up her phone and checked the ID screen, trying to keep any trace of disappointment out of her voice when she answered, "Haley. How was the date?"

"I had a great time. Kris is really nice. Very funny. There was this really cute thing he said during dinner..."

Pushing her computer aside, Anne sat back in her chair to listen to her friend's step-by-step description of last night's successful first date. She didn't mind the interruption. She and Haley had grown very close during the past couple of years, bonding through the unique stress only another medical student could completely understand, and she treasured their friendship.

Which only made her feel guiltier for not telling Haley about Liam, she thought with an uncomfortable squirm in her chair. As time had passed since they'd started studying together, it had become too awkward to admit she'd been married all along. Maybe she would confide in Haley soon. Haley would certainly keep her secret.

Anne thought it might feel good to unload. Though honestly, today she had no idea what she would say.

Haley was still chatting when the doorbell rang twenty minutes later.

"There's someone at my door, Haley. I'll see you in class tomorrow, okay?"

"Sure. See you, Anne."

Her caller tapped on the door before she could reach it, sounding impatient. "Hello? Delivery."

A delivery? On a Sunday?

She checked the peephole. The young man wore a uniform shirt and carried a huge bouquet of flowers. She opened the door.

The flowers were roses. Red, lush, fragrant, arranged in a crystal vase. The deliveryman thrust them at her, along with a gold-wrapped box. "Happy Valentine's Day."

"Thank you. Wait, I'll—"

But he was already moving away, waving off her words. "Got a bunch of deliveries this afternoon. Have a good day," he called over his shoulder.

Closing the door with her hip, she cradled the vase of flowers in the crook of one arm and carried that and the box to the table. She couldn't resist burying her nose in the blooms for a moment before setting the vase down. She loved the scent of roses. She also loved chocolates, she thought with an appreciative eye at the familiar box. She would ration those for days, savoring them for as long as they lasted. How sweet of Liam to—

Happy Valentine's Day, Anne. Love, Mom and Dad.

The card had been tucked into the roses. She stared at it blankly for a moment.

Well. Wasn't that thoughtful of her parents, to send her such a nice surprise gift? Her mother always made a point of sending her a card or something for Valentine's Day, but this was more elaborate than usual. Remembering her mom's little pep talk at the end of their last dinner together, she supposed her parents thought she needed the pick-me-up at this point in her education.

She would have to call immediately to thank them. She told herself the roses were just as lovely, the candy just as deliciously tempting as they'd been when she'd thought they were from Liam. It was petty and ungrateful to be even a little disappointed by such a nice gesture.

Blinking rapidly, she reached for her phone, a bright smile pasted on her face in the hope that it would be reflected in her voice when she spoke with her all-too-perceptive mother.

She didn't hear from Liam again until seven o'clock Monday morning. She'd just gotten out of the shower and dressed for class in jeans and a sweater and was tying off her braid when her phone rang.

Noting Liam's number in relief, she answered quickly. "Liam? I was getting worried."

"Sorry, I had some flight delays. I didn't get here until the middle of the night, your time, and I didn't want to wake you."

He sounded exhausted and…sad? "How is your father?"

The faintest of exhales sounded through the very long distance between them, preparing her for his reply. "He didn't make it, Annie. He died an hour before I arrived."

And Liam hadn't had the chance to tell him goodbye.

Her eyes filled. "Oh, Liam, I'm so sorry."

Liam's relationship with his father, Duncan McCright, had been complicated, to say the least. He'd barely known the man who'd left the country when Liam was just a child. They had reconnected five years ago—not long after she and Liam had broken up in college and had kept in touch since.

Liam had told her his father had expressed regrets at his actions after the divorce, and for the alcoholism that had separated him from his wife and his son and from everyone else who had cared about him. Duncan had been sober for ten years. He and Liam had seen each other several times during the past five and had healed a lot of old wounds. Their connection hadn't been a close one, exactly, but had been growing more so.

She'd met Duncan herself that summer before medical school when she and Liam had been together in London. Despite his flaws, she had liked Duncan very much, seeing in him many of the same qualities she'd always admired in Liam.

If only there had been more time....

The thought of losing her own dad so abruptly filled her with even greater sadness. "Are you all right? Is there anything I can do for you? Are you sure you don't need me there?"

"No, that's still not necessary. But it still means a lot that you've offered." His voice was husky with a mixture of emotion and weariness.

"You'd do the same for me."

It bothered her that both times she had offered to join him, she had suspected he would turn her down. Had that made it easier for her to volunteer? Would she have dropped everything, risked falling behind in her classes to go with him? She wanted to believe she would.

Did Liam have faith that she would have chosen his needs over her own, if she'd had to make the choice?

Pushing those concerns aside, she asked quietly, "Do you want to talk?"

"I will, later. Right now I just need to crash for a while—and you have to be in class in an hour. After I've had some rest, I'll have to deal with Dad's estate, not that there's much to settle."

"Rest well, then. Call when you have time."

"I will. I love you, Annie."

"I love you, too."

"By the way—look under your bed when you have a minute. I'll talk to you later."

He hung up before she could ask why he wanted her to look under the bed.

Wiping tears from her cheek, and swallowing a sob she hadn't wanted him to hear, she went into her bedroom and knelt to peer under the bed. She found a large white box there.

Liam hadn't forgotten Valentine's Day after

all, she realized, opening the box to find a large, pink envelope sitting on top of something wrapped in sheets of white tissue. Her name was written on the envelope. The card depicted a bouquet of roses. A sappy but sweet poem was printed inside. Beneath that, Liam had written his own Valentine's Day greeting, signing it with love.

A lump in her throat, she unfolded the tissue to reveal an exquisitely beautiful nightgown and robe set in the palest pink satin. Delicate lace decorated the bodice. She ran a fingertip along the intricate pattern, admiring the handiwork. It was a beautiful set, so very pretty that she knew she would never wear it unless he was there to admire her in it.

She clutched the delicate garments to her breast and huddled over them, sobbing in earnest now. She cried for Liam, for his loss of the father he'd only just begun to know. And she cried because she was tired and confused, facing a future that seemed to hold only more stress and conflict and uncertainty.

After several moments, she forced herself to stop crying and went into the bathroom to wash her face, leaving the gift on the bed. Despite her emotions, she had to go to class. Had to somehow hide her feelings from her friends and concentrate on her studies. That seemed to be the only productive action she could take just then.

Chapter Seven

Liam stood in a fine mist, making no effort to stay dry as he lingered in the little church cemetery, staring grimly down at the mound of dirt at his feet. A few flowers, already wilting around the edges, were arranged on the grave. The handful of mourners who had attended his father's funeral had departed. Some would gather for a late lunch at the home of his father's only sibling, Maura Magee. Liam had been invited to join them, but he'd asked for a little time alone first.

He didn't know his father's family very well.

He'd hardly known his dad. His feelings for the man were still so complicated he could barely understand them himself. Had he loved his father? Maybe, in a vague, obligatory manner. Had he liked him? Yes. More with passing time, as he'd come to better understand the demons that had driven Duncan from his home, from his family. From his son.

Duncan had been reluctant to talk much about his past, but he'd confessed to Liam a few years ago that he'd grown up with an angry, abusive, alcoholic father, that he'd been tormented by childhood classmates, that he'd escaped his problems by running away. First to another country, and then into the bottom of a bottle—many bottles. When his drinking had destroyed his marriage to the only woman he'd ever loved—Liam's mother—he'd run away again, traveling aimlessly from place to place until he'd ended up back where he'd begun. Only then had he begun to face his past, with the help of his sister and a few old friends who had still cared about him.

It had been too late to make amends with his wife, but he'd still had a chance with his son, he'd told Liam tearfully. Perhaps they could learn to be friends, if not the sort of father-son relationship he would have liked. Liam supposed they had been friends at the end.

He wished he'd had time to bid his father goodbye. To tell him that, though the old pain of abandonment was still raw, Liam had tried to understand and to forgive.

He'd missed that opportunity by one hour, he thought bleakly. One measly hour, damn it.

"Sorry, Da," he murmured, kneeling to lay the white flower in his hand on the freshly turned dirt. "I tried to be here. I hope you knew that."

He felt very much alone when he straightened. Alone in the cemetery. Alone in the world, somehow. Which was ridiculous, of course, considering he'd never had a close relationship with his father. He had more friends and business associates than he could even count. He had a wife.

Yet none of them were with him now. None of them would be there when he walked into his rarely occupied apartment back in New York.

He'd told himself he was the luckiest guy on Earth. That he had the best of both worlds. He was a footloose bachelor with a great wife. He'd had family, but loosely enough that he didn't have to worry about pleasing them or compromising for them. He had a home, but he'd been free to travel the world on a whim. He had a job most people only dreamed of, yet enough free time to pursue other dreams, like his writing. He even had a deal pending for his first book, once he got past whatever block was keeping him from tackling those revisions. What more could he want?

Pushing his hands into his pockets, he turned away from the grave, reminding himself that nothing in his life had really changed all that much. He was still a lucky guy. He could go to New York, call up some friends, spend an evening out on the town. Or he could head back to Little Rock and spend several quiet, private evenings with Anne. The best of both worlds.

He should probably go back to New York. His presence had obviously been a distraction to Anne, though she was too generous to complain. He knew she'd been worried her family would find out about him, which wasn't something he wanted just now, either. And it wasn't as if he'd gotten anything done at her place, anyway. He and Anne could get together later, after she'd finished her classes for the semester, after she'd taken the dreaded Step 1 exam in June. That was only four months away; they would both be fine on their own until they had a chance to snatch a few precious days together.

So, he would go back to New York. To his nice, small, very empty apartment there.

Yet he had the depressing feeling that making that choice would be acknowledging defeat in his marriage.

Pushing a hand through his short, damp hair, he left the cemetery with a heavy void in his chest he didn't want to contemplate too closely. He had to make a decision before he left Ireland, and he didn't have a clue what the best choice would be.

Anne parked in her apartment lot at almost eleven Thursday night after a long and exhausting study session. The group had all agreed that this cycle's material was particularly evil—so much to learn, so little time to do so. They'd barely gotten started on the information that would be on next week's test, and already she wondered how she would ever remember it all.

She glanced up at her apartment. Only one light burned in the window, the lamp she left on a timer so she didn't have to enter a dark room when she came home late. The bedroom window was dark, as she expected. Most of the apartments around hers were also dark, considering the late hour.

She'd heard from Liam only once since he'd called Monday morning. He'd called Wednesday morning to reassure her that he was fine, and still in the process of taking care of his father's affairs. He wasn't sure when he'd get back to the States, nor had he decided at that time where he would go when he returned. Though she had assured him he was welcome to come back to her apartment to continue working on his revisions, she'd gotten the impression he'd pretty much decided to go to New York. She suspected he thought that choice would be better for her sake—but maybe he believed it was the best decision for himself, as well.

She would eventually grow accustomed to his absence again, she assured herself as she trudged up the stairs. After all, he'd spent only a little over a week with her. Soon it would seem entirely normal to come home to an empty apartment, to go for days or even weeks without hearing Liam's voice. And maybe she would see him in the summer, after her Step 1 exam. Although, her rotations would begin early in July, so there wouldn't be a lot of time to spare.

Vaguely depressed, she unlocked her door and walked inside.

She paused just inside her doorway, her head cocked, her instincts on alert. The apartment was dark and quiet, as she had expected. The light from the one lamp didn't show anything out of place. There was no evidence that anyone had been inside the apartment while she was out—and yet, somehow, she sensed someone had been there.

Slipping out of her shoes, she tiptoed to the open bedroom door. The lights were off in the room, but the night-light in the attached bathroom provided just enough pale illumination for her to see the dark shape on her bed. Still making no sound, she crept closer.

Fully dressed except for his shoes, Liam lay on his side on top of the covers, as though he'd intended to lie down only for a few minutes. She could just see his face in the shadows. Even in sleep, exhaustion carved deep lines into his forehead and around his mouth. His breathing was heavy and even, telling her he slept so soundly that he was unaware of her presence.

Seeing him there, she realized that she hadn't

really expected him to come back, despite his indecision on the phone. She'd been prepared for him to call from New York to tell her he'd chosen to finish his work from his apartment there. She'd have been no more surprised had he called from Malaysia or New Zealand.

Yet he was here. In her bed. Only then could she allow herself to admit to herself how very much she had wanted him to come back.

He never stirred when she slipped into the bathroom to wash her face and brush her teeth, nor when she stripped out of her clothes and donned her nightgown. Pulling a blanket from a shelf in the closet, she spread it over him, then climbed beneath it with him.

He roused a little when she settled next to him.

"Annie?" His voice was thick, the syllables slurred.

"Yes, it's me. Go back to sleep."

"Hope you don't mind—I couldn't go back to New York yet. Didn't want to be alone now."

She touched his face, her heart aching for him. "I don't mind at all."

His voice was growing fainter. "Didn't want to leave things like they were. That stupid quarrel we had—"

"Shh." Snuggling her head into his shoulder, she wrapped an arm around him. "Go back to sleep, Liam. We'll talk tomorrow."

"Okay." He pulled her more closely into him. Barely a minute passed before he was deeply asleep again.

Anne lay awake for a while longer, staring at the darkened ceiling and listening to Liam breathe.

Liam was drinking coffee when Anne walked into the kitchen Friday morning. She wore a casual shirt and jeans, and her hair was still damp from her shower. She had applied a little makeup, not that she needed any. Apparently, she would be in classes all day today since she wasn't dressed to see patients.

"Good morning, Annie."

She smiled, though she searched his face as if gauging his well-being. "Good morning."

He bent his head to brush a kiss across her lips, all he would allow himself because he knew she hadn't much spare time. "Sorry I conked out on you last night. I meant to lie down for only a few minutes, but I guess I went unconscious. I barely remember you getting into bed with me. Or I suppose I should say, onto the bed with me. I didn't even turn the covers back when I laid down."

"You must have been exhausted."

"I guess I was."

She reached up to rest her hands on his shoulders, her expression somber now. "I'm so very sorry about your father. Are you okay?"

He gave her a gentle smile. "I'm fine. But thank you."

"If you need to talk about it, I can skip classes this morning. Haley will share her notes with me."

Touched by the offer, he shook his head. "No way. Have your breakfast and then go to class.

We can catch up when you have a few spare minutes."

"You're sure? Because—"

"Annie," he cut in, speaking firmly now, "I'm sure."

After hesitating only a moment longer, she poured herself a cup of coffee. "How was your family in Ireland? Your aunt Maura—is she well?"

"Yes, she looked great. The others were all fine, too—what few there are. Not many left of Dad's family."

Leaning against the counter, she took a tentative sip of her hot coffee before asking, "You got all his affairs settled?"

"It didn't take long," he replied with a slight shrug. "Dad didn't have much to settle. I gave most of his things away. I kept the pocket watch that had belonged to his dad, a locket that was his mother's and a few small mementoes of his time with my mother and me—pictures, mostly. Nothing particularly valuable, other than sentiment."

Her tone was sad when she said quietly, "I'm so sorry you didn't get to tell him goodbye. That must have hurt you."

He kept his gaze focused on his own coffee cup. He didn't want to upset her before her classes by letting her see exactly how much that still bothered him. "I wish I could have been there a little earlier. Aunt Maura told him I was on my way, so at least he knew I was trying. He left a message for me through her."

"Did he?"

He could tell she wanted to ask, but didn't want to pry. He didn't like that slight distance between them, that cautious hesitation that shouldn't exist between a husband and wife. "Yes. He asked her to tell me that he loved me, that he was proud of me and that he was sorry for his paternal short-comings. She said he seemed to know somehow that he wouldn't be able to tell me those things himself."

Tears glazed her eyes when he glanced up at her from across the table. "Oh, Liam—"

He managed a weak smile for her. "I'm fine,"

he repeated. "I'm glad Dad and I were able to make our peace before he died, but it isn't as if he was a part of my life even then. I've only seen him a few times since we reconnected."

"I know. But it still hurts, doesn't it?"

He nodded and reached for his coffee, then deliberately changed the subject. "What about you? How's it been going this week? Are the classes any easier than they were for the last unit?"

"No, not really. But I guess I'm keeping up."

Something in her voice made his eyebrows rise. "What's wrong?"

"Nothing."

Nope. She was still holding something back. "Annie."

She sighed. "It's just—well, something seems a little off with my study group. It's bothering me a little."

"Off? In what way?"

"I can't describe it, exactly. It just feels as though something is changing. We don't seem to be as comfortable together as we have in the past. I don't know if it's the stress getting to everyone, or what, but there's a tension that hasn't been there before. Like I said, it bothers me."

"Maybe you've all been spending a little too much time together," he suggested. "Maybe you should all take a break."

"Maybe," she agreed reluctantly. "But there's so much studying to do. And it's easier to study together than alone most of the time. Someone always has an answer when the others are stuck, or an explanation for something that's confusing someone else. One of us catches something the others miss, or has a clever method of remembering something that helps the rest of us remember, too. I don't know how I would have gotten through these past semesters without them."

"I'm sure it will pass. You've all gotten too close to let it fall apart now. Like you said, it's probably just the stress."

"I'm sure you're right." But she didn't look entirely convinced.

"You should all do something fun after the

next test. Maybe throw a party or go out for pizza and beer or something. You could have the party here. I could clear out for an evening."

She frowned. "I hate that you have to hide whenever anyone comes to my apartment."

He shrugged. "That was the agreement."

"I know. But still—"

"Don't fret about it. I knew what I was coming back to, and I'm okay with it. I'm going to dive into my writing today. I'm hoping to have it all finished in a couple of weeks. After that, well, I'll clear out and let you get back to your studies without worrying about my presence here. Unless you'd rather I go back to New York to finish? If I'm interfering at all, I want you to tell me now."

"Of course you're not interfering," she said firmly. "You've actually been a great help to me here, cleaning and cooking and doing laundry— all things you don't have to keep doing, by the way. If it's easier for you to concentrate here rather than in New York, then stay."

"Then I'll stay for a little longer," he said,

dipping into his oatmeal again, choosing to believe her, despite his suspicions to the contrary. "With all the distractions in New York, it's a lot easier to work here."

He kept his reasoning focused on his work, knowing this wasn't the time for an in-depth discussion of the state of their relationship. Anne didn't have time, and he wasn't sure she was ready for that yet, anyway. Perhaps he wasn't, either.

Maybe he had come to a gradual realization for his primary reason for marrying her—wanting to keep that strong link between them when they were apart so that they wouldn't give up as they had back in college—but it had become increasingly clear to him that he wasn't entirely certain why Anne had agreed. Nor whether she stayed married to him, despite the obstacles they had encountered, because she loved him or because her habitual avoidance of conflict extended to him as well as to her family.

He didn't want to believe the latter. He wasn't her father. He wouldn't bully her if she made a decision he didn't like. Which didn't mean he wouldn't try to change her mind, he thought with a ripple of discomfort. He tried to take comfort in assuring himself that he would be much more tactful about it than her family had ever been.

"That's settled, then," she murmured, setting her coffee cup on the counter. "You'll work here for a while longer.

"Should I make dinner for us tonight or are you eating with your group?" He kept his tone light, as if he were asking only for convenience, but he really hoped she would be free to spend a couple of hours with him that evening. He had missed her quite badly the past few days. More than he was prepared to admit to her just then because he didn't want to put pressure on her to push her studies aside for his sake.

She grimaced, and he knew before she spoke that there would be no intimate dinner for them that evening. "I'm sorry, Liam. Today's my grandfather's eightieth birthday. We're celebrating at his country club, and the family will expect me to be there."

So it was her family coming between them again tonight. It was always either that or her studies—and of the two, it was her family he resented most, rightly or wrongly. Nodding a bit curtly, he tried to keep his tone uninflected. "Of course they want you there. Don't worry, I'll fend for myself. I've got a lot of work to catch up on, anyway. Answering my backlogged e-mail, alone, will take two or three hours."

Despite his encouragement, she still looked vaguely guilty. "I wish you could go with me. I wish everyone already knew about us and the drama was all behind us and we could just walk in together as a couple, you know?"

He reached across the little table to squeeze her hand. "That time will come, Annie. Once you've finished these tough classes and aced that big exam—as I know you will—we'll break the news and damn the consequences."

Her smile was a weak attempt. "Of course we will. After I've got that behind me, I'll be ready for whatever their reactions will be. Maybe they'll surprise us and come around quickly once they know there's nothing they can do about it."

"Maybe they will."

But Liam wondered. Would her family ever really accept him when they had taken such a dislike to him all those years earlier? And would Anne ever really be prepared to choose him over them, if it came to that?

Looking very handsome in a beautifully tailored dark suit, Dr. Stephen Easton stood in front of the popular, local swing band that was providing entertainment for the birthday bash and lifted a flute of champagne. The crowd that had gathered for the celebration paused in their eating and conversations to listen as Stephen cleared his throat to signal the beginning of his toast.

Sitting at a white linen-draped round table between her mother and Stephen's fiancée,

Danielle, Anne reached for her own champagne.

"To Granddad," Stephen said in a voice that carried clearly around the room. "Dr. Henry Easton, Sr., a man who has been an invaluable asset to his community, a true leader among his peers and a role model to three generations of medical students, including his own. My father, my sister and I are among those fortunate enough to follow in his noble footsteps. Happy eightieth birthday, Granddad, and may we all be privileged to celebrate many more with you."

The praise was a little over the top, of course, a little too flowery—but Anne couldn't deny that her grandfather loved every word of it. Sitting next to his son, he beamed as everyone in the room raised a glass and sipped in his honor.

After nodding acknowledgement of the applause that followed his toast, Stephen motioned for the musicians to resume and rejoined his family at their big, round table. He shook his grandfather's hand, then his father's before sliding into the seat beside his fiancée and greeting her with a quick kiss.

"Stephen, that was lovely," their mother said in misty approval. "I'm so glad both you and Danielle were able to be with us tonight. And Anne, too, of course," she added quickly.

Anne smiled and nodded. Surreptitiously, she studied her mother's face. Her mom looked tired, but happy, she decided. She had insisted on planning and organizing this birthday celebration herself, the first big party she had put together since her stroke, though she'd certainly arranged plenty of social and charitable events in the years before her illness. Anne worried that her mom had overtaxed herself for this evening, but she figured her dad had kept a close eye on her during the preparations.

Glancing around the nearly filled room of friends, family and business acquaintances, she couldn't help noticing how many couples were in attendance. Her mom had urged Anne to bring a friend—implying that a date would be welcome—but Anne had replied lightly that there wasn't anyone she particularly wanted to bring. And there wasn't, other than Liam, whose presence would not have made the celebration a pleasant one.

She glanced at her watch, wondering how quickly she could get back home to him. She felt terrible leaving him alone like this when he'd just gotten back from his father's funeral. She could almost feel her spirit being tugged in different directions by her need to be with her Liam, her obligations to her family and her responsibilities to her studies. The result was a dull headache that just never seemed to go away these days.

Though she'd hoped to be discreet, her time-check did not go unnoticed. "Looks like Anne's eager to get back to her books," her father said with more approval than censure.

"Of course she is," Granddad replied jovially. "Don't feel like you have to waste any more time at this shindig, sweetheart. I'm glad you could come, but none of us want to interfere with your schoolwork, do we?"

Her family smiled indulgently at her, nodding their agreement.

How would those expressions change if she were to suddenly blurt out the truth about what was waiting for her at home? She wondered how they would act, what they would say. How long it would take them to forgive her, as she assumed they would, eventually.

Glancing at her mother's slightly pale, still-so-thin face, she forced a smile. "I can stay a few more minutes. At least until after they bring out the cake and we sing 'Happy Birthday.' I wouldn't miss that for anything, Granddad."

Her grandfather smiled contentedly again, basking in the attention. Maybe Stephen looked at her a bit closely, but no one else seemed to notice anything odd about her behavior. Once again, she had managed to fool everyone, she thought, wishing she could feel a little more pleased with herself and less like an ungrateful daughter and a terrible wife. Mostly, she wished she could feel less like a coward.

Still a little tired from his travels, Liam slept in Saturday morning. Anne dressed as quietly as possible, then crept out of the bedroom, closing the door soundlessly behind her. Liam had barely stirred since she'd slipped out of bed.

She was supposed to meet her study group later, but she was thinking of canceling. She could study here today, and that way she would be available if Liam wanted to talk about his dad.

He'd said he'd come back to Little Rock because he hadn't wanted to be alone in New York after his loss, she thought guiltily. And yet she had spent very little time with him since he'd returned. He didn't seem to blame her for that, but she blamed herself for not making the time to be there for him if he needed her. She could make up for that today, even if it was only to keep him company while they both worked on their own pursuits.

When she'd been rushing between classes and frantically trying to make her family celebration last night, it had fleetingly occurred to her that it would have been easier, perhaps, if Liam had gone back to New York. Yet she was still pleased that he hadn't.

Liam had a way of keeping her head spinning with conflicting emotions, she thought with a weary sigh.

She had just set up her computer when she heard the shower running. Maybe she should make something for breakfast, she thought. Liam would probably be hungry.

She gulped when someone tapped on her door. She hoped fervently that it was Rose, the only person for whom no awkward explanations of Liam's presence would be necessary.

But it was Haley who stood on the other side of the door, wearing an expression that was both harried and apologetic. "I'm sorry to drop by like this. I should have called, but I panicked."

"What happened?" Anne asked, instantly alarmed.

"My hard drive crashed. I had another one installed first thing this morning, but I didn't have all those slides from yesterday backed up. Would you let me make copies from your computer, please?" She held up a portable storage device. "It won't take long."

"Of course you can copy my files." Anne stepped out of the way to allow Haley to enter. She'd have been just as upset if it had been her computer that had crashed, she acknowledged, shuddering at the very thought. Especially now, with so much material to be memorized. "I could have e-mailed it to you, though."

"I know. But I just left the computer store, and I thought I'd just drop by. You're sure you don't mind?"

The shower had stopped. Anne hoped Liam would hear her talking with Haley and stay in the room until the coast was clear. "Of course I don't mind," she said, raising her voice just a fraction and hoping Haley wouldn't find that odd. "I just turned on the computer. We can—"

The bedroom door opened and Liam wandered out, his shower-glistened body bare except for the towel wrapped precariously around his waist. "Anne, I forgot to take my jeans out of the dryer last night. I—"

Suddenly realizing that she wasn't alone, he skidded to a halt, making a hasty grab for the loose knot of the towel.

Her eyebrows raised, Haley gave Liam a rather lengthy once-over while Anne stood there like an idiot, trying to think of something reasonably intelligent to say.

Haley was the first to recover her voice. "Well, hello, there."

Liam shot Anne a grimace of apology. He looked as though he expected her to strangle him on the spot—and she had to admit, that was an option.

She swallowed hard when Haley turned slowly toward her. Haley's eyes danced with mischief and speculation when she murmured in a suspiciously neutral voice, "Apparently I came at a bad time."

Anne sighed in resignation. "Haley, this is—"

"Lee," he supplied helpfully, obviously hoping to get away with the ruse a second time.

"Liam," she finished firmly. She'd had few qualms about keeping the whole truth from the virtual stranger who lived downstairs, but she would not lie to her best friend. "Liam, this is Haley."

Though he gave Anne a quizzical look, Liam spoke to Haley. "Oh, yes. I've heard all about you."

"Wish I could say the same." Haley gave him another look that made his cheeks go even redder as he stood there with only a big, fluffy towel covering him from waist to knees. His dark hair was still damp, he wasn't wearing his glasses and the muscles in his bare chest and arms were beautifully molded, adding up to a delicious and thoroughly masculine image. Which would have made his blush all the more amusing to Anne had the circumstances been different.

"I'll just go get dressed," he muttered, backing into the bedroom. "Please excuse me."

The door closed quickly between them. Anne suspected Liam stood on the other side punching himself in his head for his recklessness.

"Well, well." Haley set her computer bag on the floor and crossed her arms over her chest, eyeing Anne with exaggerated accusation. "Someone has been holding out."

"I have," Anne admitted, "but it wasn't because I didn't want to tell you. I just didn't quite know how."

"You didn't know how to tell me that you're sleeping with that gorgeous guy from TV? Gee, I can't imagine why."

So, Haley had recognized him—and Anne had confirmed the identification by giving Liam's real name.

"It's even more complicated than that, I'm afraid." She drew a deep breath before blurting, "Liam is my husband."

Chapter Eight

As if her knees had given way, Haley sank onto the nearest chair. "Your…husband?" she repeated, obviously wondering if she'd heard correctly. "You're married?"

"Yes." Anne cleared her throat. "Let me get you a cup of coffee and I'll tell you all about it."

"Coffee. Yeah, I could use coffee. Black."

Anne nodded. "I'll be right back."

As she pulled coffee mugs from a kitchen cabinet, Anne tried to decide how to explain to her friend that she'd been hiding her marriage for almost two years. And then how to convince Haley to behave in front of their other friends as if nothing at all had changed. It wasn't that she thought Haley would reveal her secret deliberately, but there was no doubt that this news changed everything Haley thought she had known about Anne.

If only she'd had time to prepare. To decide whether to keep Liam's presence secret or to introduce him to Haley less...dramatically.

Haley accepted the mug of coffee, then held it between her hands without tasting it as she watched Anne settle on the couch with her own mug. "I know you weren't expecting me this morning," she said. "If this is a bad time, we can talk later."

Anne shook her head. "I've been wanting to tell you, anyway. I was just waiting for the right time."

"Waiting for me to show up on your doorstep and meet the hubby in all his, um, glory?"

Anne had to laugh at the ironic query. "No, that wasn't exactly the plan."

"Well, I can't say I'm sorry I got that delectable eyeful." Haley made a show of fanning her face with one hand. "The man is seriously hot."

Hearing herself giggle like a schoolgirl, Anne felt her own cheeks warm. She drew another deep breath, telling herself to get a grip.

"So, how long have you been married?"

Anne replied almost apologetically, "A little over a year and a half. July tenth will mark our second anniversary."

They had spent their first anniversary on separate continents, she recalled fleetingly. Liam had been filming in Bangladesh. He'd been able to call, but their conversation had been all too brief and dissatisfying. It had been another month before they'd managed a long weekend together in New York—one of those covert escapes she had pulled off without anyone being the wiser that she'd even left the state. She was still amazed at times that they'd been able to keep their secret this long.

Liam reappeared just then, fully dressed now in a polo shirt and khaki cargo pants, his hair dried and neatly combed, his glasses perched on his nose. He looked at Anne a bit warily, as if wondering if she were mad at him for his lack of caution earlier. "Is there any more of that coffee?"

"Yes, it's still hot."

While Liam fetched his coffee, Anne filled Haley in about the details of her unannounced marriage. Even after he rejoined them to sit on the couch beside Anne, Liam said little, letting Anne choose how much to reveal. She couldn't tell how he felt about her confiding in her friend. His expression was politely neutral during the conversation.

Haley looked a little confused when Anne finished speaking. "So, let me get this straight. The two of you dated in college, but your parents made you break up with him?"

Liam nodded. "Yes."

"No." Anne frowned at Liam. "That wasn't why we broke up in college."

He lifted an eyebrow at her. "Of course it was.

They said I was holding you back, distracting you from your studies."

She shook her head. "Liam, we didn't break up because my parents made me. You wanted to drop out and tramp around the world doing your travel reporting. I wanted to get my degree and go to medical school."

"I believed at the time that you didn't really want to go to medical school, that you were just doing what your parents wanted you to do. The year you took to study abroad after college proved me right, you weren't ready to go straight into medical school then."

She shook her head. "That had nothing to do with what happened between us. We simply agreed that we just weren't in the right places in our lives to maintain a relationship."

"That's not quite how I remember it," he murmured.

Perhaps she'd made it sound easier than it had been. Less traumatic. She remembered a few heated discussions, plenty of tears—but she'd always believed the decision, while hard, had been mutual.

Haley studied them both. "Then you ran into each other by accident in London when you were studying abroad, Anne?"

"Yes."

This time it was Liam who replied, "No."

Anne blinked at him. "What?"

"I knew you were there," he said with a shrug. "Heard it through the grapevine, you could say. I made sure we ran into each other."

Thinking back to that seemingly random encounter in a Chelsea fish and chips place, she stared at him in astonishment. "You found me intentionally?"

"Um—yeah."

"And why, exactly, did you not tell me this before?"

He shrugged. "I guess it just never came up."

Haley choked on what might have been a muffled laugh. "Do you two ever actually, you know, talk?"

"We haven't really been together all that much," Liam admitted with a wry look at Anne. "During our entire marriage, we've spent only a total of maybe four weeks together—two of them in this one visit. Most of our conversations have been on the phone or through e-mails."

Haley's smile faded. "That has to be tough. And I understand why you didn't feel like you could spring the news on your family when your mother was so ill, Anne. But she's a lot better now, isn't she?"

"She had a troublesome setback last year, but on the whole, she's doing much better now."

"So, why don't you tell them? Wouldn't that be easier than all this sneaking around?"

Anne and Liam looked at each other quickly, and then away. "It's just not the right time," Anne muttered. "You know how tough school is right now. Not to mention that we're about to have to start studying in earnest for Step 1. My family would be in such an uproar that I couldn't possibly concentrate on my studies."

"And I'll have to leave again in a few weeks,

anyway," Liam added, sounding as though he agreed completely with her on this point, at least. "I'm staying here only until I finish writing a book about my travels, then I'm taking off for Haiti in a couple of months to report on the orphaned street kids there. I'd hate to leave Anne to deal with the fallout of our announcement by herself. It would be better to wait until we can live together openly."

It was the first Anne had heard about him going to Haiti. Was this a new development for him, or had he simply neglected to mention it before? Haley was right, she realized abruptly. She and Liam really didn't communicate enough.

Not to mention that he seemed no more eager to break the news about their marriage than she was.

"So you're just going to go on the way you have been?"

Anne and Liam shared quick glances, then nodded in unison.

"For now, anyway," Anne said.

"It seems best," he agreed.

After a moment, Haley shrugged. "Whatever works for you. You can both be assured that no one will hear the truth from me."

Anne smiled at her. "Thank you, Haley. I knew we could trust you. I wish I'd told you sooner. It bothered me to keep it from you when you and I have become such good friends. I hope you can forgive me."

"There's nothing to forgive," Haley replied immediately. "You had your reasons. Nothing at all has changed between us. Except I guess I'll have to stop trying to fix you up with guys," she added with a laugh.

"I'd appreciate that," Liam said wryly.

Propping her chin in her hand, Haley studied Liam openly. "You look really different with the short hair and the glasses. It's no wonder you haven't been recognized around here."

"How did you recognize him?" Anne asked curiously.

This time it was Haley's turn to blush. "I'm a huge fan. I've seen all your TV episodes. I recognized you as soon as you stepped out of the bedroom—even if you weren't wearing your usual safari gear," she added with a little giggle. "As soon as Anne confirmed your name, I knew I was right, as unlikely as it seemed."

He smiled, looking flattered, which made Anne tempted to kick his shin. Just because. She could all too easily imagine that he met plenty of gushing female fans—and Haley was the only one who knew he was unavailable. Anne didn't even like to think about his encounters with the ones who considered him fair game.

"Are you going to grow out your hair again?"

"Probably. As Annie has pointed out, the hair's more famous than I am," Liam said with a laugh.

"Oh, I doubt that. It's your talent that's gotten you where you are. You make all your reports so interesting and so informative. Sometimes I feel almost as if I'd visited those places myself after I've watched one of your shows."

"Thank you. That's what I hope to accomplish."

Haley glanced at Anne. "It must be hard for you to sit here in this apartment studying while Liam's off seeing so many fascinating places."

Anne forced a smile. "I'm doing what I have to do to pursue my own career," she said with a light shrug. "Liam has his dreams and I have mine."

Something about that statement didn't sound right, she thought after she'd said it. Too much "his" and "mine" and not enough "ours," maybe. But since that was the state of their marriage for the time being, there was no use fretting about it.

She stood rather abruptly. "We should start transferring those files you need, Haley. It won't be long before we have to go meet the guys for our study session."

"And I should get to work myself." Liam stood and smiled at Haley. "It was a pleasure meeting you, Haley. Anne, I'll be in the office if you need me for anything."

She nodded, not quite meeting his eyes as he walked away. He closed himself into the other room, leaving her alone with her friend. Fortunately, Haley seemed to sense that Anne needed to concentrate on school concerns for a while, rather than any further discussion of her complicated relationship with Liam.

While there was some relief in having her friend know the truth, Anne was beset by a sudden, uncharacteristically superstitious fear that one accidental discovery could lead to a domino effect of everyone she knew uncovering the secret she'd been trying so hard to hide for more than a year. Though at the moment, discovery seemed to be only one of the perils she and Liam faced.

As Anne had expected, Haley was entirely circumspect in front of their study group about what she had discovered. With the exception of making no more jokes about blind dates or singles' clubs, she treated Anne no differently than she ever had, making it easier for them both to pretend that nothing had changed. And yet, Anne felt that the accidental revelation had deepened their friendship. Perhaps it was because she no longer needed to lie to Haley, even by omission, which gave her the freedom to be completely herself in front of her friend. It was nice to have one person, at least, other than Liam with whom that was possible.

The group met for intensive study sessions both Saturday and Sunday afternoons. Maybe because they were so focused on their common goals, the tension Anne had been sensing among them lately seemed to ease. Even Haley and Ron stopped sniping at each other and started cooperating more with helping all of them learn as much of the material as possible.

Still, Anne believed something had changed in the past couple of months, and she couldn't quite figure out what it was. Maybe it was her own guilty conscience, she thought with a slight wince, though she didn't know why she should feel at all remorseful about keeping her private life hidden from the guys in the group. It wasn't as if she knew everything about their lives, after all.

She didn't know why Ron had grown slightly less jovial during the past few months. He was still the one who could most easily make everyone else laugh, but he wasn't quite the class clown he'd been when she'd first met him. Maybe it was just that he, too, was having trouble dealing with the pressures of classes and tests.

As for James—well, she doubted that any of them really knew James. They all liked him, they considered him a real friend, an important part of their group—but there were parts of James that he kept hidden from all of them. She and Haley had discussed that a couple of times when they were alone, wondering idly together what made James so obsessively private. They'd decided it was none of their business, really, and they chose to like him, anyway, just as Anne believed he genuinely liked all of them.

If she could respect his boundaries, why should she feel so uncomfortable about having one rather significant secret of her own?

They ended their session at just after five Sunday afternoon, because several of the group had other plans. Anne and Haley paused by Anne's car for a moment before going their own ways.

"I dread Daughtry's lecture tomorrow," Haley confided in a grumble, continuing a conversation they had started inside. "He was so boring last week, it was all I could do to stay awake."

"Not to mention all those snide comments he made about how if we were too stupid to understand all the material he was throwing at us, we'd never pass Step 1 and we'd all wash out of med school."

"I know, right? He was just in an all-round lousy mood that day."

Anne was aware of that, but it hadn't stopped her from being stung by the instructor's grim warnings, even though they had been addressed to the whole class equally, and certainly not to her personally.

"How are things at home?" Haley asked in a

furtive voice, changing the subject after looking around to make sure no one else could hear them. It was the first time she'd asked about Liam, even indirectly, since she'd left Anne's apartment Saturday, probably because this was the first time they'd been alone since.

Anne wrinkled her nose. "I haven't been there much to tell. You should know. We spent all day studying with the group yesterday until late last night."

And there came the guilt again, she thought, squirming a little. She should be spending more time with Liam, especially since he had just lost his father. But he had insisted she meet with her group, as she would have had he not been there. He was fine, he kept telling her. Busy with his revisions, which he still seemed reluctant to discuss with her.

"No more unexpected visitors?"

Laughing a little, Anne shook her head. "No. Our secret is still safe."

"Was Liam upset that I barged in that way and saw him there?"

"No, I don't think so. He enjoyed meeting you."

"So he's been here a few weeks and I'm the only one who has recognized him?"

"He wears a ball cap pulled low when he goes out in public. But, yes, as far as I know, you're the only one who's identified him."

"I've seen his photo in a few magazines," Haley confessed. "I've been intrigued by his career since I first discovered his cable program while flipping channels one night a couple years back. Everything about him just seems so… larger-than-life, I guess. On TV, anyway."

Amused, Anne asked, "Not in person?"

"Oh, he's still interesting in person. Still seriously good-looking. He was just, well, more normal than I expected him to be. I mean, married and living in your apartment and doing laundry and working in your office rather than tramping through some exotic location."

Anne bit her lip. Was that part of what Liam had worried about? That being seen as a settled, married man would make him less interesting to his viewers, and as a result, to his sponsors?

"So, when are you going to tell your family the truth?" Haley asked curiously. "Have you decided on a particular occasion?"

"Not really. We keep waiting for the right time, but we haven't actually defined what that time would be. The longer we wait...well, the harder it is, you know?"

"I can imagine. It would be tough enough to announce a new marriage to your disapproving family, but if they find out you've actually been married for more than a year..."

Anne gulped. "You see why it's so complicated."

"I guess. Liam's okay with waiting? He isn't pushing you to tell your family soon?"

"He's in no more of a hurry than I am. He's not looking forward to the mayhem, either. And he has his career to think of. He's the footloose, bachelor adventurer, remember? He has to consider how this news would affect that image."

"It would make headlines," Haley conceded.

"At least in certain venues. Some of the gossip columnists might be intrigued that the adventurer chose a quiet, brainy medical student from Arkansas as a mate. How will you feel about being photographed and interviewed with him, with people wondering about whether you're a suitable match for him?"

Anne shuddered. "Gee, thanks, Haley. Just what I need to give me nightmares tonight."

Haley looked instantly apologetic. "Sorry. I was just speculating. It's not as if Liam's a rock star or anything. You wouldn't be surrounded by paparazzi or anything like that."

But Haley was right that there would be some media attention given to Liam's marriage, Anne reflected glumly. Especially when his book was published to add to his public image. And, being the private type she was, she wasn't looking forward to that scrutiny.

She and Liam hadn't even talked about that part of the future—like so much else that they'd avoided discussing or planning. How had she ever let herself get into this crazy situation? Was it really only because she hadn't wanted to upset her parents during her mother's health crisis? Because of her own stress over the first two difficult years of medical school? Or was there more to their hesitation to go public? Were they holding back because neither of them was really sure the marriage would survive if they tried to make it more authentic? More "normal?"

Haley being who she was—unafraid to broach the more difficult topics—asked carefully, "Um, you don't suppose there's any other reason Liam wants to keep the marriage secret, do you?"

Anne didn't have to ask for clarification. "If you're talking about other women, I trust Liam completely," she said, trying to speak with total assurance.

After a moment, Haley smiled wryly. "That either makes you very confident in your man—or incredibly naive. I'm not sure I could be so trusting."

But then, Haley probably wouldn't have gotten into a situation like this to begin with, Anne thought glumly, making an excuse to be on her way. As she drove the short distance back to her apartment, she told herself that she did trust Liam as far as other women were concerned. But could their marriage survive the other obstacles between them—his antipathy toward her family, and theirs toward him, his constant traveling and her commitment to her career training, the parts of themselves they had never fully revealed to each other? Her answer to that nagging question didn't come as easily to her.

She tried to push her worries aside and put a smile on her face when she entered her apartment. She had an entire evening to spend with Liam. Even if she would use part of that time for studying, there was no reason they couldn't set aside an hour or so for…

She stopped short just inside her apartment door. "Um—what's going on here?"

Liam was on his hands and knees in the middle of the living room floor. A squealing toddler straddled his back, somewhat sticky-looking hands clutching Liam's hair.

Liam grinned ruefully up at her. "Hi, Annie."

"Horsie!" Little Parker kicked his bare feet insistently into Liam's sides, making Liam wince and then rear obligingly up on his knees, pawing the air with his hands and making whinnying noises. Parker shrieked in delight, the shrill sound driving itself into Anne's eardrums like a shard of glass.

She raised her voice a bit to be heard above the tiny cowboy's laughter. "Is Rose here?"

"Rose is at work. Her aunt had to cancel babysitting services at the last minute this evening, so Rose begged me to fill in. She promised it would be just this one time."

The rather breathless explanation was punctuated with whinnies and more squeals, but Anne followed along easily enough. She could picture the scene— Rose had probably been desperate and tearful and Liam couldn't say no. She suspected she might have done the same under the circumstances, despite her better judgment.

She crossed the room to set her books and

computer bag on the table, pushing them to the center to make sure they were out of a toddler's reach. "When will she be back?"

"She said she gets off work at nine. So she'll be here shortly after that."

Anne glanced at her watch. Another three and a half hours? Really? What were they supposed to do with the child until then? And how would she ever get anything done with Parker here?

"The horsie needs a rest, Park-o," Liam said, smoothly rolling Parker off his back and onto the floor. He rose a little stiffly, scooping the toddler onto his hip at the same time. "Don't worry, Annie, I'll keep the kid occupied. I'm going to feed him dinner and then take him down to his place for b-e-d. Rose gave me her key. She said he's usually out cold by eight."

"She gave you her key?" Her young neighbor was certainly the trusting sort, to leave both her child and her key with a man she'd met only a couple of times, she thought disapprovingly.

Liam shrugged. "I've talked to her a few times when our paths crossed outside. Played with Parker a bit in the courtyard. I guess she figured she could trust me by now."

She didn't realize he'd gotten quite so friendly with the duo. She supposed he'd been lonelier than she had realized here by himself so much. "Oh. Well."

"Play, Lee," Parker insisted, tapping Liam's cheek for attention.

"Okay. How about we play with the farm set you brought with you?" Liam carried Parker to the other side of the room, where a thick canvas bag was propped against the wall, next to a brightly colored red plastic barn. Distracted by the sight of Parker, Anne hadn't noticed those things before. She watched as Liam sat cross-legged on the floor and opened the hinged barn, shaking out cartoonish plastic animals, a tractor and trailer, and a big-headed farmer. A moment later, noisy and improbable animal sounds came from that direction as Liam and Parker enthusiastically shuffled the herd into the trailer.

Liam glanced around at her with a smile. "Maybe you should study in the office," he suggested. "If you close the door, the noise won't be so disturbing."

He was making it clear that he didn't expect her to help him with the favor he'd taken on. She appreciated his consideration. Glancing at the office doorway, she thought about taking him up on his suggestion, but then she shook her head. "I'll make dinner while you entertain Parker. What do you think he would like to eat?"

"Hmm. What do you like to eat, Park-o?"

Giggling in response to the nickname, the child answered cheerfully, "'Ghetti."

"Spaghetti?"

He nodded eagerly. "'Ghetti."

Thinking of the mess to come, Anne swallowed hard and turned toward the kitchen. "Okay. Three orders of 'ghetti, coming right up."

Liam laughed.

Somehow Anne ended up spending almost an hour on the floor with Liam and Parker after their messy, ultracasual meal. They played with the farm animals and with some plastic kitchen utensils and pots and pans from Anne's kitchen. Parker pretended to cook for them, and they made a show of eating the imaginary food, to his delight. Anne was surprised by how much she and Liam laughed during the game; she wouldn't have thought playing with a toddler would have been so entertaining.

When Parker began to yawn, Liam glanced at his watch. "I'll take him down," he said, gathering their "toys." "Rose told me where to find everything."

"You're sure you don't need help?"

"I've got it covered, thanks. I'm sure you're ready to get back to your books."

She wondered what his friends and associates back in New York would think if they heard that a young single mom had asked him to watch her toddler, having no idea who Liam really was. And that Liam had shown no more fear of being responsible for a two-year-old than he did of the wild animals he encountered on his program.

He made her feel like such a coward sometimes, she mused after he'd taken Parker down to bed. It seemed sometimes as if she was over-whelmed by everything, whereas Liam feared nothing. Just one more item to go on the list of differences between them, she thought, her smile fading.

She was buried in her studies again when Liam returned a little over an hour after carry-ing Parker off to bed. She glanced up and smiled faintly when he entered. Tossing the book he'd taken to read while Parker slept onto a table, he sank onto the couch with a gusty exhale.

"Did you have a hard time getting him to sleep?"

"Not really. He was worn out. I know the feel-ing. Toddlers are exhausting. I don't know how Rose does it by herself."

"She has her aunt to help her, but you're right, for the most part she's on her own. I know she must have been grateful for your help this evening."

Liam grimaced. "She offered to pay me, can you believe that?"

"I'm sure she didn't know how else to express her appreciation."

"Sorry to have cut into your study time this evening. I didn't know how to tell her no. I guess I could have watched him down in her apartment, but I didn't really want to mess around in her kitchen for dinner."

"It's fine, really. He was on his best behavior. I enjoyed spending time with him."

"Yeah, it was kind of fun, wasn't it? Not that I'd want to do it very often," he added with a crooked grin.

He pushed himself to his feet and moved toward her. "I'll go answer e-mail for a while and let you get back to work. But first…"

He leaned over to place a long, hard kiss on her mouth. "Thanks for cooking the 'ghetti," he murmured when he finally released her.

Turning abruptly, he headed for the office. "Don't study too late," he said over his shoulder. "You need your rest."

Blinking, she shook her head a little to clear her fuzzy mind and made herself look at her computer. The fact that it took her a moment to remember how to read was entirely Liam's fault.

Chapter Nine

Liam was growing concerned about Anne the next evening. She'd told him she should be home around ten, but it was more than an hour past that time when he looked at his watch. It wasn't like her to be out this late when she had ICM the next morning, and she had told him that she did.

He tried to focus on his revisions, but they were still proceeding with painful sluggishness. He still couldn't figure out why he was having so much trouble finishing this project, though he found himself wondering if he was subconsciously stretching out the work as long as possible. After all, once he'd finished the book, he really should go back to New York and to all the projects he'd left hanging there.

While there was some grain of truth in that excuse, he knew it wasn't the only reason for his difficulties. He just couldn't quite identify the other problems.

Giving up on any attempt at working, he began to pace, trying to convince himself that it was foolish to worry about Anne. Her hours were always erratic, and it wasn't unusual for her study group to lose track of time as they plodded through all their material.

He spent a few minutes wondering how other spouses and significant others of second-year medical students dealt with being pushed to the background so often. When they weren't actually in class or buried in their books, med students seemed to be frequently tense and distracted and moody, from what little Liam had observed. It was no wonder so many relationships broke up during these years.

He didn't want to think that his own marriage might not survive the pressure of their demanding careers.

She spent so much time with her study group. Haley and those three men, two of whom were single. They were probably getting to know each other very well. They had so much in common. He pictured her studying and laughing and teasing with her friends, bonding through pressure with them in a way outsiders would probably have a difficult time understanding. He remembered how fondly she had smiled when she'd talked about having to hide chocolate cake from her buddy, Ron. Were she and Ron sharing a late, sweet snack at that moment?

He pushed a hand through his hair in irritation as a surge of savage jealousy crashed through him. That was uncalled for—and totally unlike him. As much time as he spent away from Anne, they had to trust each other or they might as well give up now. He was just letting his worry about her get out of hand.

But he still didn't like the thought of her being so chummy with those other guys.

His cell phone beeped to signal an incoming text message. Snatching it from its holder on his belt, he read the terse note. Hide. Dad w me.

"Great." Shoving the phone back into its case, he glanced around the living room to make sure there was no evidence of his presence, then moved into the bedroom and closed the door, wondering what Anne's father was doing with her at this hour. How long would he have to cower behind the door this time, holding his breath and hoping he wouldn't be discovered?

Though Anne had assured him that she rarely had visitors, this apartment had been a very busy place during the past few days.

He found it grimly interesting that he was not particularly relieved to find out that Anne was with her father, rather than her single male study buddies. Liam was well aware who was most likely to come between himself and Anne—and it wasn't her chocolate-loving pal.

He'd been in the bedroom less than ten minutes when he heard the door open in the other room.

"Just set that bag down on the floor, Dad," he heard Anne say. "Thanks for bringing it up for me."

"You shouldn't carry so much stuff around in your car," her father replied, his voice clearly audible through the thin bedroom door. "It's not a rolling closet."

Anne laughed ruefully. "I know. I kept meaning to clean it out, but I just never seemed to find the time."

"How are you going to get to class tomorrow? Do you need me to come get you?"

"No, that's not necessary. I'll catch a ride with Ron or James. My apartment is on the way for both of them."

Liam felt his eyebrows lower into a scowl.

"You can't get by without a car," her father scolded. "Nor do you need to be distracted from your studies by trying to deal with this. I suspect that the repairs on your engine will be expensive—more than the car's worth, most likely—not to mention time-consuming. Let me buy you a new car. I'll pick one out tomorrow and have it delivered to you tomorrow afternoon."

"No, Dad, you aren't buying me a new car." Anne's voice was firm. "If I need a new car, and I won't know that for certain until I hear what the mechanic says, I'll take care of it myself. I still have my savings, and I have enough in student loans to cover a modest car payment. I told you when I started medical school that I wouldn't let you support me financially, and I meant it. I'm an adult. I intend to act like one."

"Fine." Her father sounded annoyed. "Consider it a loan, then. When you've finished your surgical residency and you're making a good salary, you can pay me back. With interest, if that makes you feel better."

"As if you'd let me. Please, let me handle this. I really appreciate your help tonight, but I can take it from here. I'll call if I need anything else, I promise."

He argued a few more minutes, but Anne was

resolute. She escorted him out with reminders that it was late and that her mother would be worried if her dad didn't get home soon.

Liam waited until he heard the door close, then another couple of minutes just to be sure Easton was gone.

"Liam?" Anne opened the bedroom door, both looking and sounding weary. "I'm sorry about that. I barely had time to get a text message to you without alerting Dad what I was doing."

"No problem. I heard most of what you said. What happened to your car?"

"It died," she answered simply, spreading her hands. "Just sputtered and quit at a traffic light. I couldn't get it restarted. Dad thinks it's serious. He had it towed to his mechanic, who will look at it tomorrow and give me an estimate."

"You called your dad?" Liam tried to keep his tone neutral.

"Yeah. Like I said, I was stranded at an intersection. I'm just glad there weren't many other cars there at that hour. The ones that passed by were able to go around me. A couple of people stopped as if to help, but I waved them on. Fortunately, Dad arrived quickly, so I didn't have to sit there long."

"It never occurred to you to call me?"

A small frown creased her brow. "I'm sorry. Were you worried because I was so late?"

"I didn't mean you should have called me to tell me you'd been delayed," he answered impatiently. "I was asking why you didn't call me to come get you. To help you with the car problem."

He could tell by the rather blank look on her face that the idea had never even occurred to her. "I guess I just thought automatically about my dad because he had his mechanic look at the car a couple of months ago when I had some problems with it. He arranged tonight for a tow truck to take the car back to the same mechanic to find out how extensive the damage is this time."

"I see."

Anne looked at him with confusion in her

eyes. "Liam, are you actually annoyed that I called my father instead of you?"

"Your daddy instead of your husband, you mean?"

Maybe that came out a little snippy. Anne planted her hands on her hips and tipped her head, her eyes narrowing. "And just what was that supposed to mean?"

He shrugged. "I'm just saying. It seems a little odd that you'd call him, especially knowing you'd be lectured the whole time you were with him. And even though by having him bring you home, you were taking a risk that he might notice something that would make him suspicious about us."

"I knew you would stay out of sight when I sent you the message. I wasn't too worried about Dad seeing anything."

She seemed to be worrying less and less about her family discovering their secret. Was she getting overconfident—or was there a part of her that almost hoped they would be found out? "I still think you should be more careful. I'd have come for you, and I'd have helped you get the car towed. Your family wouldn't have had to even know about it until you got around to telling them."

"I know you would have been happy to help. It's just that Dad has always helped me when I had car problems, so I guess it was simply out of habit that I called him tonight."

"It's that sort of habit that keeps you under your family's thumbs," Liam muttered. Even he didn't quite understand why it stung him so much that Anne hadn't even thought to turn to him when she'd had a problem. Maybe he had more male ego than he'd realized, especially when it came to his wife.

And if he didn't shut up, he was going to end up sleeping on the couch tonight like the stereotypical husband in the doghouse, he thought with a wince as Anne's face flushed with anger. Judging by the glint in her eyes, he'd be lucky if he didn't end up sleeping on the sidewalk.

"I am not under my family's thumbs," she said, very slowly and deliberately. "I live on my savings and my student loans. I pay my own bills and make my own way. Perhaps I ask my family for advice or minor assistance occasionally, but that doesn't mean I am dependent on them. I could have arranged my own tow tonight, if necessary, and found my own way home, but I knew Dad wouldn't mind helping out."

"Damn it, Anne, you should be letting *me* help you. Let me pay for the repairs or buy you a new car. We're married. My money is your money."

"I don't see it that way," she replied defensively. "Especially since no one even knows about our marriage. I don't need my family to take care of me—and I don't need you to do so, either. Considering how rarely you're even in the same country, I'd say it's a good thing I *can* take care of myself."

That little barb hit its target. Liam shoved a hand through the hair he'd chopped so he could spend time with her. "You knew when we married that my job would involve this much travel. You said you didn't mind, that you would be too busy with medical school to spend much time with me, anyway."

"And that's still true," she said, though her tone was rather flat. "So don't blame me for not being in the habit of calling you for assistance with the kind of minor issues that occur in my regular routines here."

"I'm not blaming you," he muttered, conflicted emotions tangling inside him. "I just don't understand why you complain about your family's interference in your life and then you choose to turn to them when you have a problem. Every time you're around them, you come home looking even more pressured, but you still go back to them whenever they summon you."

"They're my family. I love them. And they love me." She shook her head in apparent exasperation as she snapped her response. "Just because you weren't close to your parents doesn't mean I should become estranged from mine."

Maybe something showed in his face that he didn't intend to let her see.

"I'm sorry," she said after a brief, taut pause.

She took a step toward him and laid a hand on his arm. "I'm sorry. That was a terrible thing to say to you, especially now."

He didn't like seeing the tears gathering in her eyes, and knowing he was responsible for them. "It's okay," he said gruffly. "You're right. I wasn't particularly close to my parents."

"Not through any fault of your own. You were only a child when your father left and your mother died. It was unforgivable of me to use that against you. I'm sorry."

"I'm the one who should ask for forgiveness." His stomach tied in hard knots, he reached out to brush a tear from her cheek with the pad of his thumb. "You're exhausted. It's been a very long day and you're trying to get ready for the test Friday. I promised you I wouldn't add to your stress while I'm here, and what did I do? I snarled at you because your car broke down and you took care of it without my help. I'm sorry."

She sniffled and shook her head. "I still shouldn't have spoken to you that way."

He forced a smile. "We could stand here apologizing to each other all night. Let's agree to put it behind us, shall we? Why don't you go freshen up and I'll make you some chamomile tea to help you relax before bed."

She nodded and drew a shaky breath, looking as relieved as he was that the quarrel was over—at least for now.

Fortunately, the car repairs were not extensive as Anne's father had feared. Relieved that she wouldn't have to deal with buying a new one until summer, at least, Anne drove a loaner car arranged by the mechanic until she got her own back Wednesday afternoon. Though he offered, she refused to allow her dad to pay for the repairs. She was still stinging over Liam's words Monday evening, even though they had been almost formally polite to each other ever since.

It seemed to be the week for conflict. As Friday's test drew closer, the tension in the study group mounted. They argued about the best ways to study for the tests, they disagreed on some of the slide interpretations, they even quarreled once about where they should meet to study. Saying he was tired of sitting in various kitchens, Ron suggested a coffee shop or the library, while the others asserted there were fewer distractions in someone's home than in a public place.

Attempting to analyze was what going on with the group, Anne decided that burnout was taking its toll on them all. They hadn't had a break since Christmas. The weeks had passed in a blur of classes, lectures, clinical lessons, study sessions and exams. The instructors were beginning to harp more and more on the looming Step 1 exam, which merely added to the dread already gripping the class. The students were all dazed and sleep deprived. It was no surprise they were so tense and snappy. Nor any wonder that so many relationships had suffered—marriages, romances, friendships, even study groups.

She tried not to blame her group's problems solely on Ron and Haley—after all, they had all snarled occasionally—but she had to admit that Ron and Haley, in particular, were taking out their anxiety on each other. She still didn't quite understand their relationship—was there an attraction, did they just rub each other the wrong way or did they simply not like each other? Whatever the issue, she wished they could set their differences aside long enough to get through the rest of the semester. She depended so much on the encouragement and support of this group; it already made her sad to think they'd be splitting up next year and going into separate rotations.

Thursday evening, the night before the test, was particularly distressing. None of them—with the possible exception of James—felt completely ready for the exam and they had several differences of opinion about what facts they should be focusing on in their studies that evening. Each had a different idea of what topics would be covered most heavily on the exam. They ended up splitting up early for the evening, each going to their individual homes to study on their own.

Sensing that Anne was upset, Liam was particularly supportive that evening. He kept fresh tea in her cup, saw that she had fruit to munch on for quick energy, even quizzed her on some practice questions. He didn't even nag her—much—to get some sleep when he finally turned in after midnight, leaving her still awake, promising him she just wanted to look over "a few more things" before she joined him. It was after one when she finally gave up and succumbed to sleep.

As was her custom after an exam, she returned to her apartment drained and bone-tired, heading straight for her bed for a nap.

She woke to the scent of roses. Before she even opened her eyes, she inhaled deeply, letting the soothing fragrance waft through her. When she finally blinked and pushed herself upright, she was greeted with the sight of a dozen gorgeous orange roses in a crystal vase on the nightstand.

Delighted, she buried her nose in the cheery bouquet and inhaled deeply. Only then did she see the new dress she hadn't yet had a chance to wear draped over the chair in the corner of the bedroom. A note lay on top of the draped skirt. *A fancy night out or a casual night at home? Your choice.*

She had to smile at his wording. He'd obviously made plans for the evening, but he wasn't entirely sure she would be in the mood to go out. She picked up the dress and slipped into the bathroom.

Fifteen minutes later, she had freshened her makeup, pinned up her hair and donned the dress, accessorizing it with her grandmother's diamond necklace. She wondered what Liam had in mind for the evening.

He waited for her in the living room. Dressed in a dark suit with a crisp white shirt and a deep red tie, he held a white rose in his hand. Her heart nearly stopped at the sight of him looking so very handsome.

He presented the rose with a little bow that

made her come very close to a girlish giggle. "You're wearing the dress. Does that mean you're in the mood to go out?"

"I would love to get out," she assured him. She assumed he would take the usual precautions about not being recognized. She thought the short hair, glasses and conservative suit would go a long way toward that end. He hardly resembled the wild-haired adventurer who was most often seen tramping through jungles and wading through muck.

She couldn't decide at the moment which side of Liam she preferred.

He had made reservations at an exclusive and expensive Little Rock restaurant. They dined in a secluded, romantically dim corner lit only by the table's candles and one ruby-shaded sconce light. Soft music filled the room, underscoring the suitably restrained conversations around them, making the dining experience even more intimate. This, he told her when she expressed her pleasure at this nice surprise, was the dinner he had planned to share with her on Valentine's

Day. She felt as though that holiday had been held over just for the two of them this year; she couldn't imagine a more perfect way to celebrate.

Liam advised her not to order dessert at the restaurant, giving her a hint that there was more in store for her. Rather than taking her straight home after dinner, he drove across the Arkansas River into the city of North Little Rock, where he parked in the lot of a traditional Irish pub she had always wanted to visit, but had never found the time.

Stepping into the pub, which had been built in Scotand and imported to Arkansas, was like going back in time to their summer abroad. The gleaming woods, the amber pendant lights, the smells of stout and stew. The sound of Celtic music being played by a quartet in one corner, and of darts hitting boards in a back room. The conversation here was louder, more raucous than at the restaurant. The accents were more Southern than Gaelic, but Anne could still pretend they were back in Scotland.

She felt herself going rather misty and she blinked rapidly a couple of times before turning to Liam with a smile. "Let me guess. You want a Guinness."

He grinned. "Of course."

They jostled through a rather tipsy group to find a table near the window where they could watch pedestrians, cars and trolley cars pass outside. Liam ordered a pint of Guinness and chocolate mousse cake; Anne requested half a pint and bread pudding. They lingered over their desserts, laughing and talking and reminiscing, never once mentioning her classes or her squabbling friends or her family or their own uncertainties. Anne thought she knew now why she'd always found an excuse not to visit this particularly local establishment. She couldn't imagine being there without Liam.

Their desserts were down to crumbs in the bottom of the serving dishes when she excused herself to visit the ladies' room. She wasn't gone long, but by the time she returned, some other woman had already invaded her territory.

Pausing across the room, she watched with narrowed eyes as an attractive young blonde with well-displayed assets flirted with Liam. Did the woman recognize him? Or was she simply making a move on a strikingly handsome male sitting alone in a booth—and not wearing a wedding ring on his left hand?

She slid into her seat with a brilliant smile for Liam. "Did you want coffee before we go?"

The blonde drifted off with a sigh of resignation. Liam chuckled and tossed some cash on the table. "No, I'm ready to leave if you are."

Anne glanced sideways. "A fan?"

"No. Just a friendly local."

"Mmm." A little too friendly in Anne's opinion, but since Liam was already grinning at her, she said no more about the incident.

By the time they finally arrived home, she was pleasantly tired and utterly relaxed. "That was such a beautiful evening out," she said to Liam when he closed and locked the front door behind them. "How did you know it was exactly what I needed tonight?"

He smiled and walked across the room to turn on the MP3 player she kept in a speaker dock. Even that move had been planned, apparently. The music that drifted from the speakers wasn't from her usual playlists; Liam must have loaded some romantic instrumental numbers just for tonight.

He took her into his arms in the middle of the living room, swinging her into a slow, sensual dance. Wrapping her arms around his neck, she followed easily, her hips moving with his. "Why, Mr. McCright—I do believe you're trying to seduce me."

His teeth flashed in a smile. "Is it working?"

Pressing her breasts against his chest, she almost purred against his throat, "I believe it is."

She loosened and removed his tie as they danced. He let down her hair. Still swaying to the music, she slid his jacket from his shoulders and tossed it aside. He unzipped her dress.

The music seemed to follow them as they drifted toward the bedroom, leaving a trail of clothing behind them. Liam didn't bother turning on the light. Falling onto the bed with him, Anne wished very hard that she could make this perfect night last for a very long time, keeping all the problems of daylight far away from them.

Anne was already at her books when Liam came out of the shower late the next morning. Rather than sitting at the table, she had spread out on the couch this time, her computer in her lap, her bare feet propped on the table in front of her.

He leaned over the back of the couch to brush a kiss against her cheek. "You look exceptionally beautiful today. Just as you do every day."

Tilting her clean-scrubbed face toward him, she motioned toward her ultracasual T-shirt and jeans. "You must have spent too much time in the Irish pub last night. You're full of blarney this morning."

He laughed and circled the couch to sit on one arm to chat with her for a minute before he tried to get back to his own work. "I don't think I asked before—are you meeting with your group today?"

"No, we're taking the weekend off. We're all studying on our own this weekend. We need the break from each other."

"I can see why you would. Do you get a spring break this semester?"

She made a face. "Yes, in mid-March. And we have an exam the day we return, followed immediately by a practice Step 1 exam that we have to do well on or be forced to sign up for a review class this summer. Then in April, we start 'shelf exams'—end of the semester tests for each subject. So, basically, we spend all of spring break cramming for regular exams and shelf exams and trying to find time to prepare for the Step 1 exam. It isn't exactly a vacation."

So much for his vague plan to whisk her away somewhere, just the two of them, for the week off from classes. "And when do you start your third-year rotations?"

"The beginning of July. I'll have maybe two weeks off after Step 1."

"July." He nodded, making a mental note to clear his calendar for those two weeks. "Okay, maybe we can plan something for then. Think you can slip away to join me somewhere exotic and romantic—and private? You could tell everyone you need a vacation, and surely they will understand that. They wouldn't have to know you won't be spending that vacation alone."

"I'll see what I can do." After a moment, she set her computer aside and turned on the couch to face him more fully. "You know, I've been thinking."

Something about her tone warned him that he might not be quite comfortable with what she was going to say. "Thinking about what?"

She moistened her lips and twisted her hands in her lap. "I think maybe we should start thinking about ending this silly charade of ours."

His first, instinctive reaction was that she was suggesting they end their marriage, and that was like a hard punch to his stomach. She had told him how perfect last night had been, and she had certainly shown her appreciation—twice—afterward. Why would she want to end things now?

Which left only one explanation. "Um—charade?" he asked nervously.

"You know what I mean," she said, her expression impatient now. "All this sneaking around. Hiding behind doors and under the brim of baseball caps, jumping every time the doorbell chimes. We never intended to keep our marriage a secret for this long. I think we should start discussing how and when we should make the announcement."

"You're ready to tell your family the truth?" he asked, startled.

He could see the nerves in her darkened eyes, in the lines around her mouth, in the taut set of her shoulders, but she gave a little nod. "I'm getting there. Not immediately, of course. I still think it would be best to wait until after Step 1. But maybe before that July vacation together. What do you think?"

His stomach clenched again and his skin felt clammy. His physical reaction was a bit stronger than he might have expected, but he tried to keep his expression composed when he asked, "I'll be filming then, but I can probably take a little time to join you here if you think the time is right to break the news to your parents. But are you really sure you'll be ready for that right before you begin your third-year rotations?"

Though she looked nervous at the prospect, she gave a little shrug. "I could deal with it. Probably. I'd just tell my parents that I don't have time for family drama. If I tell them they're interfering with my studies, I'm sure they'd back off. Their biggest fear is that I'll wash out of medical school, so they wouldn't do anything to upset me overly much. Probably."

Which all sounded well and good, but he knew it wouldn't be that easy. Besides, she wasn't the only one who would have to deal with her family once their marriage was no longer a private one.

"I'm pleased that you want everyone to know

about us," he assured her, though a tiny, accusing voice inside him whispered that he lied, making him feel like a jerk. "But we shouldn't make any rash decisions. We need to think this through before we do anything we can't take back. You know, make sure it's the right time, and that we're both ready to go public."

Her eyes darkened. "I'm tired of the lies, Liam. It just gets so frustrating."

"I know, babe. But the main problem is, you're just tired. You're running on fumes, and this is totally the wrong time to set yourself up for more problems. Let's just wait until summer, okay? It's not that much longer."

She studied his face with narrowed eyes. "You make it sound as if you aren't in any hurry at all to tell anyone. Is it because of your career? Or are you actually content to go on the way we have been?"

Good questions, he acknowledged. And he had no real answers for her. Because he hadn't been expecting her to suddenly suggest they announce their marriage, he hadn't really thought about when they would get around to making their announcement. "I just think it's a bad time for you, Annie. Focus on your studying for now, and we'll deal with everything else when you're got the worst part behind you."

She shrugged. "Fine. If that's what you prefer."

She picked up her computer again and settled it in her lap. "I guess I should get back to my studies."

"Anything I can do to help? Want me to quiz you?"

"No, thanks. I have a lot of reading to do today."

He nodded and pushed himself off the arm of the couch.

He hadn't handled that very well, he thought as he moved slowly toward the office. It seemed to him as though a light had gone out in Anne's eyes that had been there when they'd awakened this morning. Maybe it was just the reminder of all she had to do within the next few months.

Or maybe, he thought with a hard knot in his

chest to match the one in his stomach, she had been hoping for something from him that he hadn't quite known how to offer her.

"I never had a chance to ask—how was your weekend?" Haley asked when she and Anne finally had a chance to speak in private Monday. It had been a very busy morning filled with classes and other obligations and neither of them had even had time for a lunch break. Anne had offered Haley a lift home because Haley had taken the bus to the campus that morning. Haley had eagerly agreed, giving them an opportunity for a brief chat session during the short drive to Haley's apartment.

"It was fine," Anne replied, keeping her eyes on the traffic ahead of her. "I got a lot of reading done for this week's classes. How was yours?"

"Not bad. Kris and I went out Saturday night. We saw a movie, had a few drinks. It was fun."

Anne glanced sideways toward her passenger. "You really do like him, don't you?"

Haley shrugged. "Like I said, he's a nice guy and he makes me laugh. If you're asking if I've started falling for him yet, the answer is no, not really. If he never called again, I wouldn't stew about it. As busy as we stay, I'm not sure I'd notice for a few weeks."

Anne wondered if Kris was as casual about the relationship as Haley. He seemed to be awfully patient and persistent for a man who was only an occasional companion.

"What about you?" Haley asked. "Did you and Liam do anything interesting?"

Anne thought she should probably be amused by the exaggerated stealth of Haley's tone—as if anyone else could hear them in her car. Yet, she found little to laugh about in the situation. "We went out Friday night, after the exam. We had a very nice dinner, then went to that Irish pub in North Little Rock for drinks and dessert afterward."

"Sounds like fun."

"Yes, it was."

"You needed that. Just like I needed to go out Saturday night."

Anne nodded. "I wore my new dress. The one I bought when you and I went shopping."

"Oh, the coral one. It looked great on you. Did Liam like it?"

"I believe he did." Even though he had been eager to peel her out of it once they'd returned home, she thought with a ripple of remembered heat. She didn't bother mentioning that part to her friend.

"I bet he enjoyed going out with you. He's been spending a lot of time cooped up alone in your apartment."

"Yes, he has." Which had been his own choice, Anne reminded herself when guilt threatened to nibble at her. "And he did seem to have a good time."

"How's he doing with his writing? He's been here—what? Three weeks?"

"Well, he arrived three weeks ago, but he spent almost a week in Ireland when his father died."

Haley nodded somberly, having been filled in on that sad detail. "Is he doing okay with that?"

"He doesn't talk about it." It was one of several topics Liam seemed to be avoiding. Like his writing. And their future.

She braked for a red light, then glanced toward Haley. "I, um, suggested to Liam that we tell my parents the truth as soon as I've taken the Step 1 exam," she said, feeling a need to confide in her closest female friend. "I think maybe the time will be right by then."

Haley's eyes went wide. "Wow. You're really ready to tell everyone?"

Anne nodded rather glumly. "Almost. We had such a beautiful night Friday, and I woke Saturday morning not wanting that feeling to end. I guess I just wanted everyone to know that Liam and I are together."

Especially pretty blondes in random bars, she thought grimly, then winced. She really hoped there was more to her wish to finally take that big step than simple jealousy. It wasn't as if she wanted to take an ad out in the next day's paper; she just thought it was time she and Liam began to discuss going public.

"Did you and Liam decide how you're going to make the announcement? Are you going to tell your family on your own, or will he join you?"

"We didn't get that far in our discussion." She cleared her throat, then admitted, "Liam didn't think it was a good time to talk about it. I could tell the suggestion caught him off guard. And not necessarily in a good way."

"What do you mean?"

"He said it was a bad time for me to make any decisions, with all the other stress I'm under. Classes and tests and everything."

"He has a point there." Haley looked suddenly weary as she rubbed the back of her neck with one hand. "I can hardly find time to eat and sleep, much less make any important decisions not connected with the next exam. Let's face it, we're all stretched pretty tightly."

Anne nodded. "I know. It was just—"

Haley studied her perceptively. "Just what?"

The light turned green and Anne turned her attention toward the road ahead as she mentally groped for words. "Liam didn't seem all that impatient to announce our marriage," she murmured finally. "I got the impression that he wanted to put that off as long as possible."

"I see." Haley hesitated a moment before asking, "Why do you think that is?"

Anne smiled wryly. "You aren't a shrink yet, Haley, but you're already talking like one."

Haley shrugged a bit sheepishly. "I still haven't decided for sure that I want to go into psychiatry. But the question remains. Why do you think Liam doesn't want to make the announcement?"

"I don't know." She'd given that question a great deal of thought in the past couple of days. She hadn't liked many of the possibilities that had occurred to her.

"I can think of one significant reason he'd want everyone to think he's single."

Anne shook her head in response to Haley's

gentle suggestion. "It has nothing to do with him wanting to see other women," she insisted. She was completely confident about that. Well, maybe ninety-nine percent confident, she thought with a slight frown.

"Is it his job? Does he think he's a more interesting celebrity as a bachelor?"

"Maybe—even though he always refuses to talk about his personal life in interviews. He wants to keep the conversation on his travels and his experiences, not on his broken home or his father abandoning him when he was a kid—or his marital status."

"Makes sense. But it sounds to me as though he's mostly worried about you. I'm sure once the semester is behind us, he'll be very proud to tell everyone the two of you are together."

Anne supposed Haley was right. It wouldn't be much longer until summer, she reminded herself. Which, of course, meant that it wouldn't be long until the Step 1 exam.

"What time are we meeting to study tonight?"

she asked, deliberately moving her attention to the more immediate concern.

Anne and Liam met for an early dinner at a popular Chinese fast-food place not far from the campus Wednesday. They had hardly seen each other that week, and Liam had been cooped up in the apartment for days, so they both needed the break.

The place was crowded, as always, and Anne couldn't help worrying a little that she would run into one of her classmates, but Liam was dressed very incognito again. His preppy polo shirt and jeans were far from his usual safari gear, his hair was freshly trimmed and he wore the ball cap again, which he didn't bother to remove for the casual surroundings. He wasn't the only one wearing a cap while eating. They had agreed that if she did see someone she knew, and if introductions seemed called for, she could simply refer to him as her friend Lee.

Conversation was made somewhat difficult by the noise level of the dining room, but they managed to make small talk as they wound pad Thai noodles on to disposable chopsticks. Liam looked rather happy with the amount of work he'd accomplished that day.

"It's going better, I take it?" she asked, pleased that he seemed satisfied with his results.

He nodded. "I think I've finally figured out my strategy for easing from one story into the next. It seems to be flowing well now. I should be able to wrap up a rough draft by the end of next week. I'll send that to my editor for input before I spend much more time on it."

"The end of next week," she repeated, hoping the background noise concealed the hollowness of her voice. "Wow. That would be great progress."

He nodded. "After all the delays, I really have to put the pressure on now. I've got a couple of meetings scheduled in New York the week after that, and it would be a lot better if I get this project out of the way first. At least, this part of it."

So. She had a timetable now. Liam would be

leaving in approximately a week and a half. Still longer than he'd planned to stay when he'd arrived almost a month earlier, but it still seemed so soon for him to be off again.

"I'm glad it's going well for you," she said, stabbing her chopsticks into the bowl of noodles. "I was beginning to get worried, for your sake."

"You should have known better," he chided good-humoredly. "I always work things out eventually."

"That's true."

"Guess you'll be glad to have your place back. Your friends are probably wondering why you haven't invited them over to study lately."

She tried to smile. "Maybe a little. Haley keeps jumping in to volunteer her apartment whenever we're not meeting at one of the others. She's really been covering for me."

"I'm glad you have such a good friend in her. I like her."

"Yes, so do I, obviously." She watched as Liam

pushed his bowl aside after eating less than half the dish. "Is that all you're having?"

"I'm not very hungry. My stomach's been a little queasy today. Maybe a stomach bug or something."

"There's a nasty stomach virus making the rounds. Maybe you should see a doctor."

His grin was mischievous—and more than a little suggestive. "I've been seeing a doctor quite regularly. And enjoying every bit of what I've seen."

Her cheeks warmed. "I meant a real doctor—one who's already taken and passed all these stupid tests."

"I'll be fine. Don't worry about it."

"If it's not better by tomorrow, I'm going to start nagging," she warned him.

He laughed. "I read somewhere that married men tend to live longer because their wives nag them into seeing doctors. If it makes you feel better, I'll check with a doctor if my stomach is still bothering me by Friday."

She agreed to the compromise with a nod. It

probably was just a virus, in which case there wasn't much a doctor could do. Antibiotics were useless—even counterproductive for viruses, which tended to resolve themselves within a week or so. She was probably just being overly concerned, a typical med student's reaction when family fell ill.

She glanced at her watch and grimaced. "I'm sorry to have to run, but I'm supposed to meet the group at Ron's in twenty minutes."

"Of course. I don't want to make you late. I'll walk you to your car."

They stood and moved together toward the door. Halfway there, a rowdy toddler darted out in front of them, almost tangling in Anne's feet. Liam steadied her with an arm around her shoulder while the child's father captured the runaway with a murmured apology.

Anne smiled up at Liam, and he tightened his arm around her as they shared a laugh at the near collision. And then they looked toward the door again.

This time Anne almost fell over her own feet

when she stumbled to a shocked halt, causing Liam to bump into her.

"Now what?" he asked with a chuckle.

His smile died when his gaze followed hers.

Anne's parents and grandfather had just walked into the restaurant.

Chapter Ten

An hour after leaving the Chinese restaurant, Anne still felt a little shaky whenever she thought about how very close to disaster she and Liam had come. She could hardly believe they'd managed to blend into a crowd of college-age students leaving the restaurant just as her family had entered. She and Liam had both ducked their heads, and Liam had instinctively sheltered her by keeping himself between her and her parents. Somehow they had gotten out without a painful and public confrontation.

"That was entirely too close," Liam had said as they stood beside her car.

"You're telling me." She'd swallowed the hard lump that had formed in her throat when she'd seen her father. "I knew Dad liked eating lunch here occasionally, but I had no idea they were coming here for dinner this evening."

"Let's get out of here before they spot us," he'd suggested, opening her door for her. "I'll see you back at your apartment later. Have a good study session."

He hadn't even kissed her as he'd all but shoved her into her car. The near miss had seemed to scare Liam even more than it had her.

As a result of that close call, she was a bit on edge when she met with her friends that evening. And she wasn't the only one. Even though the next test was a week and a half away and they'd all had a few days' break from each other, the tension remained within her group when they gathered at Ron's downtown loft apartment. And this time she placed the blame directly where it belonged—on Ron and Haley.

"All right, guys, stop it," she insisted after Haley snapped at Ron for the second or third time that evening and Ron sniped back. "This is really getting out of hand between you two."

"Seriously," Connor agreed, looking relieved that someone had brought up the subject. "I haven't seen this sort of juvenile squabbling since I quit teaching high school. What's going on with the two of you?"

Haley scowled. "I just get tired of him turning everything into a silly joke. This is serious. Maybe it doesn't matter to you if we all pass the next test, Ron, but it matters very much to us. We have to focus."

"I'm just trying to lighten everyone up a little," Ron argued. "All we do is study and drill. It doesn't hurt to laugh every once in a while."

"And I just happen to be the most convenient butt of most of your jokes?" she retorted. "Gee, thanks. That really makes our study sessions more entertaining for me."

"Maybe if you wouldn't be quite so sensitive…"

"I'm not being sensitive! I'm just tired of you always picking at me. Making fun of my quirks, belittling anyone I happen to date, teasing me when I miss a question..."

"Oh, yeah, like that ever happens. When's the last time you were less than perfect on anything, Ms. Genius?"

James cleared his throat, the quiet noise sounding oddly loud in the sudden silence. "That's hardly fair, Ron."

Ron turned on James, then, his usually smiling eyes dark and grim. "I can see why you'd think so. You're at the damned top of the whole class. It all comes so easily to you. I don't know why you even bother to study with us."

"As it happens, I enjoy the companionship," James replied evenly, his tone a bit too patient, as if he were keeping his own temper under control with an effort. "And, yes, I need to study as much as the rest of you."

Ron snorted.

Growing more uncomfortable by the moment with the direction their conversation had taken,

Anne noticed that Connor was eyeing Ron intently.

"Ron," Connor asked quietly, "are you under the impression that you are any less valuable to this study group than the rest of us?"

Ron flushed. "Let's face it, guys, you've all been carrying me for almost two years. All of you are so smart and so damned prepared for this career. I don't even know how I got into medical school, and it's all I've been able to do just to keep up so far. I'm not at the top of the class—I have to struggle just to stay somewhere in the middle. It's going to take a freaking miracle for me to pass Step 1 and move on to third year. I don't even know what I want to do when—or if—I get this degree."

He held up his hands when everyone started to speak at once, his expression both embarrassed and chagrined, as if he'd been provoked into revealing much more than he had intended. "Don't start throwing reassuring platitudes at me. I don't need to be patted on the head. I'm just saying that if I act like none of this really matters to me, it's because I just want to be prepared in case I screw up and have to find some other career. If you all agree with Haley that I'm more of a liability than an asset to the group, then I'll start studying on my own. I'll understand."

Haley appeared to be near tears. "I never said you were a liability."

Ron glanced at her with patent skepticism. "You made it clear enough."

Anne drew a deep breath and stood. The others still sat around Ron's round table, and they all looked at her in surprise when she rested her hands on the table and leaned forward, looking from one to the other of the faces turned her way.

"Every single one of us contributes to this group," she said firmly, focusing now on Ron. "We *need* you to make us laugh, Ron. We need Haley to keep us motivated, and Connor to use his teaching skills to make some of the material easier to understand, and James to keep us calm and centered. We're all exhausted. God knows none of us has had a full eight hours sleep in longer than we can remember. We're all worried about next Friday's test, not to mention the shelf exams and the Step 1. I suspect even James worries about that, though he doesn't let us see it."

James nodded shortly. "I'd be a fool not to worry about passing that exam. None of us is guaranteed to sail through it without a hitch."

"Exactly. Which is why we have to stick together," she continued, fierce determination coloring her voice now. "I need you guys. All of you. I would not have been able to get through these past two years without you. I can't imagine preparing for these exams during the next four months without you all. But we're going to have to stick together. Haley, stop taking everything so personally. And Ron, if you don't feel like you're prepared for the next test, then for God's sake, stop fretting about it and say so! That's what we're all here for."

Haley bit her lip, looking somewhat abashed by Anne's uncharacteristic lecture. And then she peeked at Ron from beneath her lashes. "I'm sorry, Ron. I had no idea you feel like you've been struggling. It just didn't seem to matter that much to you."

"It matters," he muttered. "And I'm sorry if you feel like I've been picking on you. I was kidding around—like I do with everyone. I'll stop, I promise."

Haley nodded, but Anne noticed she didn't look particularly happy about Ron's offer.

"Maybe we should get back to work," Connor suggested. "We'll all feel better when we've gotten through the last of today's lecture slides."

Anne took her seat again, even as Ron sprang up from his own. "I'll make fresh coffee. Who, besides me, needs a cup?"

"I'll help you," Haley offered quickly, a bit too courteously. Without actually looking at Haley, Ron nodded to accept her assistance.

Anne supposed it was a start.

Gathering her things, Haley spoke to Ron, "I'll see you tomorrow?"

He nodded. "Yeah. Tomorrow."

Hesitating only a moment, Haley pivoted and moved toward the door. "Are you coming, Anne?"

"Yes. I'll be right behind you."

Anne waited until Haley stepped out before speaking quietly to Ron. "I hope I wasn't out of line earlier. I didn't mean to come down on you like a disapproving mother."

Ron grimaced. "I guess I deserved it. I was acting like a whiny kid."

"No. You were acting like a scared and stressed-out medical student. Trust me, I know all about that."

He pushed a hand through his sandy hair that was in need of a trim, his gaze focused uncertainly on her face. "You really worry about passing the tests? As well as you've done so far?"

"I'm scared every single time," she replied simply. "I come from a whole family of surgeons, remember? If I fail, I'll never hear the end of it."

His smile was crooked. "Yeah, well, I come from a family of ne'er-do-wells, and I'd never hear the end of it, either. They've all been predicting from the start that I would never make it all the way through medical school."

Indignant on his behalf, she said firmly, "They're wrong."

He reached out to give her a hug, and because the gesture was both natural and unmistakably brotherly, she hugged him in return. "Thanks," he said, looking a little sheepish when he drew away.

"Just don't forget that our group needs you," she told him a little mistily. "Good night, Ron."

"We need you, too. Every group of rowdy kids needs a mom." Tugging her braid, he smiled more naturally. "Good night, Annie."

His teasing use of the nickname startled her a little, though she tried not to show it as she let herself out. No one except Liam called her that, and it felt odd hearing it on someone else's lips. She had a feeling Liam would not be pleased to hear Ron speaking to her so familiarly, though she could assure him in all candor that she felt nothing for Ron except affection.

Liam was the only man who would ever hold her heart.

The lights were burning in her apartment when she parked in her space and climbed out of the car, drawing her coat more snugly around her as a cold breeze slithered down her collar. A hint of impending rain hung in the air, which already felt damp against her cheeks.

Shivering, she gathered her books and computer bag and headed for the stairs, toward those welcoming lights.

Having heard her key in the door, Liam stood in the open bedroom doorway to greet her when she walked in. She wondered if he was still battling that stomach bug. He looked a little pale, and his voice sounded rather strained when he spoke. "You're home early."

She nodded and set down her things. "Long night. We got through today's slides, though.

And I think we had a breakthrough, in a way, in the group. We sort of cleared the air and passed around apologies. I think we'll all get along better now."

"I'm glad to hear that. I know it was bothering you. You need the support of your friends now."

"That's what I told them." She pulled the band off the end of her braid and loosened her hair. "Are you still feeling sick, Liam? Your color doesn't look quite right."

He shrugged. "I've had some nausea since dinner, but I think it's passing now. Still fighting that bug, I guess. I hope you don't get it. You certainly don't have time to be sick right now."

She laughed wearily, though she made a mental vow to get him to a doctor the next day if he wasn't feeling better by then. "Tell me about it. I've been obsessive about washing my hands. Maybe I'll get by without catching it."

"I hope so."

"I'm going to wash my face and put on some

pajamas and spend a couple of hours going over my notes before bedtime," she said, moving toward the bedroom doorway where he still stood. He moved aside to allow her past him. "Maybe we could have some soothing tea or something before—"

She came to a sudden stop when she saw the bags sitting beside the bed. She turned slowly to face Liam, her heart beginning to thud in dread. "Are you going somewhere?"

He stood very still, his face grim, one hand pressed against his stomach. "I'm going back to New York. My flight leaves at five-forty in the morning. I hate to disturb you that early, so I'll bunk on the couch for a few hours, then head out at about three-thirty in the morning or so."

She tried to process what he was saying. "Is there some sort of problem there? Are you coming back after you've taken care of it?"

"There's not a problem in New York," he said, his voice very gentle. "The problem is here. I think it's time for me to go."

She reached out blindly, groping for support. Her hand fell on the top of the dresser, which she gripped tightly. "I don't understand."

What might have been impatience flashed through his eyes. "I don't see how you can say that after what happened at the restaurant tonight."

"Nothing happened. My family didn't see us."

"No. But it was pretty much a miracle that they didn't. Do you know how bad that would have been if we'd come face-to-face with them there? Maybe no one else in the place gave a damn who I was, but do you think your dad would fail to recognize me?"

She swallowed hard. "No. Dad would have known you right away."

"Damn straight he would. And he'd have blown a gasket right there in front of everyone."

"He wouldn't have caused a public scene." Anne wished she could be a bit more certain of that statement. "He wouldn't have wanted to embarrass my mother that way."

The mention of her mother made Liam's face tighten even more. "That was the first time I've seen your mom since her stroke, you know. It's no wonder you've been so protective of her. She seemed very…fragile."

Anne moistened her lips. "She's stronger than she appears. She always has been."

"That may well be, but I'm not going to be the cause of her having a setback. I'm clearing out before the inevitable happens. It was foolish of me to think I could live here with you and not have anyone find out. We've just been lucky so far. Especially lucky tonight."

"So, we'll tell them. We'll tell everyone," she said rashly. "I told you I was almost ready."

He shook his head. "You don't really mean that. The timing is still all wrong."

Shock began to morph into anger. Letting go of the dresser, she planted her hands on her hips. "I'm beginning to think you're the one who is so anxious to keep our marriage a secret. Why is that?"

He frowned. "We've gone over the reasons a hundred times. Your family. Your studies…"

"Yes, those were our reasons originally. But I can't help thinking you're using my excuses to camouflage your own. Why do you *really* want to keep this secret, Liam? Is it your career? Are you afraid being married will negatively affect your fame in some way?"

"I don't worry about fame," he muttered, both arms crossed over his stomach now.

"Of course you do. That's the career you've chosen. While it might not be something I seek, I do understand that publicity is an important part of your job. But other TV hosts and travel writers are married, and it doesn't seem to hold them back."

"I'm not concerned about that," he repeated stubbornly.

"Maybe you have more personal reasons for wanting to be seen as an eligible bachelor."

Temper darkened his narrowed eyes to charcoal in response to that pointed suggestion. "Are you implying that you don't trust me, despite the promises I've made to you?"

"The promises you've made in secret," she shot back at him.

"Damn it, that has nothing to do with it. I don't break my word."

"Is that it? Are you feeling trapped by those promises? Is that the real reason you don't want to tell anyone? Because you don't want to go through a public breakup like your buddy Cal Burlington?"

"He's not my buddy, and he's got nothing to do with us! You're the one who asked me to keep this marriage a secret less than a month after we exchanged vows. I've lived up to my part of the bargain. You knew when I arrived that I wouldn't be staying long. I've already been here longer than either of us expected when I arrived. Why are you acting so surprised that I've decided it's time for me to go?"

She drew a deep breath, trying to calm herself. She supposed Liam asked a reasonable question. They had agreed from the beginning that he wouldn't stay long. And yet…

And yet she hadn't expected him to leave so abruptly. To spend his last night there dozing on the couch so he could leave before dawn the next morning.

Before she could form a reply, her phone rang. Glancing at the clock, she saw that it was just after nine when she pulled the phone from its holder. She grimaced when she saw the number displayed on the screen. "It's my father."

"Of course it is," Liam muttered, and turned away.

She didn't take the time to ask him what he meant by that. "Hi, Dad."

"Are you at home? Am I interrupting a study session?"

She pushed her hair out of her face. "No, I just walked in a few minutes ago. What's up?"

"Actually, I'm calling because of a talk I just had with your mother. I could tell something has been on her mind tonight. When I asked, she said she was sure she'd seen you at the restaurant where we had dinner tonight. She thought you were there looking very cozy with a man, but when she turned to make sure it was you, whoever it was had already gone."

"I, um—"

"I might not have thought much about it, but I ran into Mike Haverty at the club earlier this week and he said he saw you out with some man at what appeared to be a romantic dinner for two last Friday night. Are you dating someone you haven't told us about?"

Several possible answers whirled through her mind. The truth. A carefully worded prevarication. The very valid response that her personal life was none of her father's business at this stage.

She'd thought she'd set that sort of boundary when she'd moved out on her own, insisted on handling her own finances and other business affairs. Yet here he was calling her and grilling her about who she was seeing, just as he had when she was in high school. And in college, she recalled with a scowl, thinking of all the heated arguments they'd had about Liam then.

She chose to respond with a combination of all of the above. "I do go out occasionally, Dad. I'm an adult, remember?"

As if her words had given him a clue to the reason for the phone call, Liam paused in the act of moving away and turned back toward her with a searching look. She shook her head to indicate that it was okay, she was handling this. He didn't leave.

"I know you're an adult, but I'm also well aware of what your schedule is like right now. With your classes and pending exams, I find it hard to believe you have many free evenings for socializing. You'll have plenty of time for that sort of thing after you pass your licensing exams.

"Although, of course, you'll be quite busy with rotations for the next two years, and the first year of your residency will be very demanding. A surgeon's schedule makes it a challenge to maintain relationships, as you know from my own example, but you're still very young. You'll have plenty of opportunities later to find someone who will understand the demands on your time. Someone like your brother found. Perhaps another surgeon."

He was planning her entire future for her, she thought with an exasperated shake of her head. Scheduling a romance for her—preferably with another surgeon—some five or six years in the future. "Perhaps you'd like to find someone for me, when you think the time is right, of course? Maybe you'll even let me meet him sometime before the conveniently timed wedding you arrange for me."

"Now, Anne, there's no need to take that tone." Her father sounded rather startled by her atypical sarcasm. "I'm simply trying to give you advice, as a caring parent. I've been through surgical training, and I know exactly how demanding it is, and how hard it is to sustain outside relationships while going through that hard schedule. I'm just trying to spare you some of the mistakes I've made in life."

"I appreciate your concern, but I'm going to have to make my own decisions. My own mistakes. I will always value your advice, but it's still my choice whether to follow it."

She drew a deep breath, then blurted, "I haven't even decided for certain that I want to be a surgeon. Maybe during my rotations I'll find another field of medicine I'll want to pursue instead."

It was the first time she'd admitted that she was considering other options. To her father— even to herself. The closer she got to having to decide what sort of doctor she wanted to become, the less certain she was that surgery was the answer.

"Of course you want to pursue surgery." He seemed stunned that she would even consider any other path. "You have a real gift for it, inherited, I'm sure, from your grandfather and me. Sam Burkhaven told me he was very impressed with you so far."

She supposed she should have been surprised her father had sought out her preceptor, but she wasn't really. He'd have taken the position himself had he been allowed to do so with his own daughter. If it were up to her dad, he would be supervising every step of her education to make sure it met his expectations.

"I'm not ruling it out. I'm just saying that the final decision is mine. And when I make that decision—when I make *any* decisions regarding my personal life—I'll expect you to acknowledge my right to do so, and to support me in whatever choices I make. I think that's a fair request."

"Of course I will always support you, Anne. Just as I always have," he added stiffly.

It was amazing how blind people could be about their own behavior, she mused with a faint sigh. She looked at Liam as the thought crossed her mind.

"Just keep in mind the things I've said to you tonight," her father couldn't resist saying. "If you are dating someone, I hope you've made it clear to him that your career has to come first now. This guy isn't the reason you're suddenly having doubts about surgery, is he?"

"No, Dad. I'm the only one making the decisions about my career."

"Good. Because boyfriends come and go, so you should always be in control of your own life. I've raised you to be an independent, self-sufficient woman who doesn't need a man to take care of her."

"Yes, you have." She almost added that she didn't need him to do so, either, but there was no need to hurt his feelings when he was only acting out of concern for her best interests.

Maybe she'd drawn her boundaries a little more clearly during this conversation; more likely, she would have to do so many more times before he finally got the message. Especially when she finally informed him that she was a married woman, and had been for quite some time—if that day ever came, she thought glumly.

"I need to go," she said, trying not to sound too abrupt. "I have some more studying to do tonight. I'll talk to you later. Tell Mom not to worry about me. I'm fine."

"Maybe you should come for dinner this weekend. I think we should talk some more about all of this."

"We'll see. Good night, Dad." She disconnected before he could say anything else.

"Did they see us?" Liam asked as soon as she set her phone aside.

"Not exactly. Mom thought she caught a glimpse of me. And one of Dad's friends saw us at the restaurant Friday night."

Perhaps they *had* been naive to think no one would ever see them. Except for her time away for college and the months she'd spent in Europe, Anne had lived in this area all her life, and her parents were prominent members of society. It was no surprise that she would run into someone she knew almost anywhere she went.

"What did your father say?"

She shrugged. "Just the usual paternal warnings about keeping my focus on my studies and not letting myself get distracted by romance."

Liam made a sound that was half snort, half growl. "Does he really think you're so helpless that you need him to supervise everything you do? This is exactly why I said you should have called me rather than him when your car broke down. He sees every request for assistance as an invitation for him to make all your decisions for you."

She looked pointedly at the packed suitcases sitting by her bed. "As opposed to you?"

Liam flushed, the angry color standing out against his pale, somewhat clammy-looking cheeks. "Don't compare me to your father."

"Why not? You're both so certain you know what's best for me. When I need to study, when I need to go out, when I need to eat or sleep, even when I should be married—at least openly married. All for my best interests, of course. Now tell me again that you aren't like my father."

"I can't believe you said that. I have never tried to control you the way he does."

"Not deliberately, perhaps."

"Not at all," he insisted.

She shrugged, seeing no end to that particular back-and-forth argument, especially since she was growing increasingly convinced she was right.

"Do you really dislike my father so much?" she asked instead, wondering if that was the reason he was so annoyed at being compared to the other man.

"Why should I feel any other way about him?" Liam asked in seething frustration. "He hated me the minute he first laid eyes on me. He's blamed me for everything that ever went wrong in your life. If he knew I was still around, he'd blame me for the way you just stood up to him, and for any doubts you might have about following the path your father laid out for you practically at your birth. He would do everything he could to convince you to dump me now—for your own sake, of course."

She crossed her arms over her chest, where her heart ached. Liam still had his locked arms pressed to his middle, as if their conversation was causing him as much pain as it was her.

"And after we tell them the truth? That you *are* still a part of my life? How will you deal with him then?"

The question seemed to surprise him a little, as if he hadn't given much thought to that eventuality. "I don't suppose I'll have to deal with him at all," he said after a moment.

"You think he's going to throw me out of the family, perhaps? That he'll never want to see either of us again?"

"Well, no. I don't think he'll go that far. Probably. I'm sure he'll want to see you again, once he gets over his pouting that you dared to make a major decision without his guidance. But I'll still be gone a lot during the rest of your medical school experience and when I'm with you, we can do what we want, on our own terms."

"So you don't see yourself attending Christmas dinners with my parents, or birthday parties for my granddad or family cookouts in the summers or weddings and funerals and other family events?"

His eyebrows rose. "I hardly think I would be welcome to attend those events."

"Then you'll have to take steps to make sure that you are welcome, won't you? Because once you and I are openly married, my family will also be your family."

The way he almost physically recoiled from that statement made a light flash in her head. "That's the real reason you don't want to tell them, isn't it? Because having my family know about us means they'll become a part of your life, too. You're doing everything you can to prevent that."

"I didn't marry your family. I married you."

She shook her head. "That's the most naive thing you've said yet. My family is a part of me."

"Looks to me like your family causes you more pain than pleasure," he muttered. "They put so much pressure on you that you're always on edge after spending time with them. They criticize your choices. You couldn't even tell anyone about us because you didn't want to deal with their reactions."

"I still think it would have been the wrong time to tell them while Mother was in the initial stages of recovery from her stroke, but I should have told them since. I suppose I was being a coward."

She surged on before he could respond. "My parents aren't perfect, Liam. They make mistakes. But they are my family and I love them."

He cleared his throat. "I can understand that. Hell, I was fond of my dad, and he was no one's idea of a great father."

Sadness made her heart feel even heavier. Did Liam really think she would ever be content to have the same sort of distant, coolly civil relationship with her parents that he'd had with his father? "I thought you understood from the beginning that I would always be close to my family."

He pressed a hand to his stomach, as if this argument escalated the discomfort he'd mentioned earlier. "You said when you married me that you were making a choice. That you chose me over their expectations for you."

"And I did. But that doesn't mean I chose to cut them from my life. Despite dreading the initial confrontations, I always assumed they would come around eventually. That they would concede my choice of a mate and accept you into the family. But that's not what you had in mind at all, is it?"

"I guess I just didn't think that far ahead," he muttered. "You and I get along pretty well on our own. We don't need their interference."

"So you really do see it as a competition," she whispered. "You always have, haven't you? You want me to choose between you and my family."

He met her eyes from across the room without saying anything. His silence, she supposed, was an answer in itself.

She shook her head slowly. "You know what, Liam? I always believed I was the cowardly one, always worrying about failing or disappointing someone or not living up to my potential. I thought you were fearless. Nothing seemed too risky or impossible for you. You wanted something and you went after it, simple as that. I always admired you for that courage—but it worried me, too. I was afraid you would get tired of dealing with my fears. That you deserved someone as reckless and self-confident as you are."

She held up a hand when he started to speak, her heart pounding as she faced him in anger and pain. "I've come to realize lately that you aren't nearly as brave as I always thought you were. All those times you took off on your world travels? Were you really chasing adventures—or were you really running away from potential problems? My family, your own past, a real commitment to this marriage you rushed us into. Why *did* you marry me, Liam? And why do you stay married to me when you don't want to deal with everything that comes with me?"

He started to answer, then fell silent, his face pale and grim as he continued to knead his taut stomach. "This really isn't the time to get into all of that," he said after a tense pause. "We're both tired, and we're likely to say things we don't mean. I'll head back to New York so you can concentrate on your studies for now, and we'll deal with all of this after your Step 1 exam."

She wondered if it were possible to hurt any worse than she did at that moment.

"You want me to study? Fine. I'll study. That should make both you and my father happy!"

Leaving him wincing, she stormed into the office and slammed the door behind her.

Chapter Eleven

The Little Rock airport was nearly deserted at 4:00 a.m. Thursday. Most of the other early arrivals wandered through the glass doors looking sleepy and a little grumpy. The recorded messages were entirely too cheery that early in the morning, earning more than a couple of scowls in the general direction of the speakers. The glare of fluorescent lights was harsh against the predawn darkness outside.

Liam sat on a padded bench, trying to get up the energy to check his bags. There were no lines yet at the security checkpoints, so it wouldn't take long to pass through and find his departure gate. He assumed he could get a cup of coffee somewhere on the way.

His aching stomach rebelled at the very thought.

He wasn't sure what hurt the most. His stomach or his chest. And he wasn't sure he couldn't blame both pains on the way he had left Anne.

She hadn't gotten up when he'd slipped out after a sleepless few hours on her couch. He didn't know if she'd awakened with his movements or not, but if so, she hadn't said anything. He doubted that she'd had an easy time falling asleep last night; he hoped she'd manage to rest enough to get her through her classes that day.

Heaving a sigh, he reached for the handle of his suitcase, then sat back again when nausea roiled deep inside him. Damn it, he didn't need this now. He felt bad enough about the quarrel he'd had with Anne. Did he really need this stomach virus or whatever it was to make him feel even worse?

He pulled a handkerchief from his pocket and wiped his face with it. He wasn't overheated, but he felt a little sweaty. Guilty?

He scowled when the word popped into his mind. Why should he feel guilty? Despite Anne's accusations, he had made the decision to leave based on what was best for her, not for himself. He was trying to reduce her stress level, not add to it. He still shuddered whenever he thought of how close they had come to walking straight into her parents at dinner yesterday. She could deny it all she wanted, but he knew she'd have been horrified had her family found out about them that way.

He wanted to blame the pressure she was under for their quarrel the night before. Apparently, her study group had dealt with some sort of crisis last night and she'd still been stinging when she'd returned home, which perhaps explained her overreaction when she had seen his bags by the bed. Having her father call in the middle of the conversation certainly hadn't helped anything. No matter what Anne said, talking to her father always left her edgy and tense.

Which made it all the harder to understand why she wasn't eager to put some distance between herself and her overinvolved family.

Because she loved them. He scowled as the memory of her impassioned voice whispered through his mind.

His stomach jerked and he pressed a hand against it, almost doubling over from the pain. Damn. Maybe Anne had been right. Maybe he should see a doctor. As soon as he got home, he would...

Home.

He pictured the empty apartment waiting for him in New York. Was that home? Was it a home if no one was there to welcome him back? If he went to bed alone every night and woke alone every morning?

He felt more at home in a tent in some desert somewhere than he did at that apartment.

So why was he going back?

He inhaled sharply, losing patience with his

own dithering. He'd made his decision. He was going back to New York. He'd made his choice.

"You want me to choose between you and my family."

Anne had looked almost horrified when she had whispered that accusation. As if the very thought was almost more than she could bear.

He didn't like knowing he had been the one to put that expression on her pretty face.

His stomach twisted again. Guilt could be damned painful, he thought with a scowl.

Anne wasn't in the mood to meet with her study group Thursday evening. She made a flimsy excuse to Haley and decided she would study at home alone that night. Not that she expected to get much done, even though she would have the place to herself. No one there to interrupt or distract her.

How could she concentrate on slides and figures when her heart was breaking?

Was her marriage over? Had it ever really had

a chance? What had made them believe they could make a marriage work under those ridiculous circumstances?

She couldn't choose between Liam and her family. It was unconscionable of him to put her in that situation. If he really knew her, if he truly understood her, he would know she couldn't—wouldn't—be backed into that corner.

She wished she could be angry with him. Instead, she was almost numb with pain. And somehow, she had to put that aside and concentrate on her studies. It was going to take a superhuman effort.

"Hi, Dr. Easton!"

Anne stifled a sigh as she nodded in response to Rose's cheery greeting. "Hello, Rose. Hi, Parker."

The little boy grinned and waved a dirty hand at her in recognition.

"We've been to the playground," Rose said by way of explaining her son's grubby appearance. "I'm taking him in for a bath now."

"He looks like he had a great time."

"He did. I haven't seen Lee around lately. Parker always looks for him when we come out to the lot."

Anne just didn't have the energy to explain that Liam wouldn't be around again for a while. If ever.

"Excuse me," she said, hoping she didn't sound rude. "I have to make a phone call."

Rose didn't take offense easily. "Sure. We'll see you around, Doc."

Sticking her key into the lock without enthusiasm, Anne shuffled into her apartment—and then stopped cold just inside the door.

Liam was lying on her couch.

She blinked to make sure she was seeing correctly. "Liam?"

He lifted his head from the cushions. "I couldn't leave it like that."

He looked terrible. His skin was colorless, there were hollows beneath his eyes and a fine sheen of perspiration glistened on his cheeks and forehead. She dropped her things and moved quickly toward him. "You're sick."

"Yeah. But that's not the point. I didn't want to leave with you mad at me. I love you."

"I love you, too, Liam." She pressed a hand to his forehead and caught her breath. He was burning with fever.

He was curled on his left side, his knees bent and slightly drawn up. "I never meant to add to your stress. I just wanted to help."

"I know. Can you lie on your back, Liam?"

"Hurts."

"I know. Just try for a minute, okay?"

He shifted, groaning with the effort. Anne lifted the hem of his shirt to reveal his lean abdomen, muttering to herself, "McBurney's point is two-thirds of the distances from the umbilicus to the anterior superior iliac spine."

Finding what she hoped was that point, she pressed her fingers into his right side. "Does that hurt?"

"Not too—" He gasped sharply when she released the pressure. "Yeah. Yeah, it hurts. Damn."

Rebound pain. Even a second-year medical

student knew that sign. "Liam, we need to get you to the hospital. I'm pretty sure you have appendicitis."

And he'd probably been battling it for several days, she thought with a surge of guilt that the possibility had never even occurred to her before this. She'd been so caught up in her own problems and issues that she'd been all too quick to dismiss Liam's illness as a minor stomach virus. The fact that he hadn't really complained, even though he must have been suffering more than he'd let on, was no excuse.

"Stomach bug," he said with a shake of his head. "I'll be okay. We really need to talk."

"We will," she promised. "After you've seen a doctor. Can you sit up?"

He started to rise, then sank back down with a moan. "Going to be sick."

"I'll be right back." She dashed to the kitchen for a plastic bowl, then hurried back to the couch.

Liam was curled up again, his arm over his eyes. "I think it's passing," he muttered.

"I'll call for an ambulance." She already had her phone in her hand and was dialing 911.

"Don't need ambulance. You can drive me."

"Liam, you can't even stand up. I can't carry you down to the car." She only hoped the ambulance arrived before his appendix ruptured.

Anne sat perched on the edge of the waiting room chair, her arms wrapped around her middle, her heart in her throat as she waited for news. Liam had been rushed into surgery only fifteen minutes earlier, and it was apparent from the haste with which the staff had acted that his condition was serious.

Peritonitis, she thought with a catch in her breathing. If it had gone septic, Liam could very well be in critical condition.

And she'd waved it off as a "bug."

She buried her face in her hands, a low groan escaping her as hot tears filled her eyes.

"Anne? I got here as soon as I could. What's wrong?"

Lifting her damp face, she stood and threw

herself into her father's arms. "Daddy. Thank you for coming."

He hugged her tightly, obviously concerned by the tremors that ran through her. "Of course I came. You called and said you needed me here. I'll always come when you call me. What's wrong, sugar? You said you aren't hurt. That was the truth, wasn't it? I did what you asked, I told your mother that you just needed my help with something and that she shouldn't be concerned, but I can tell by looking at you that something is very wrong."

"No, I'm not hurt."

"Is it one of your friends?"

She bit her lip before saying, "You're going to be angry with me, Dad, and that's okay. You have every right to be. Just don't yell at me right now, okay? I need your help."

Looking thoroughly confused, he drew back enough to search her face. "Why on earth would I be angry with you?"

"You asked yesterday if I've been seeing

someone?" When he nodded, she blurted, "I have been seeing someone, Dad. It's Liam."

He stiffened. "Liam— You mean that McCright boy?"

Clinging to his shirt, she nodded. "Yes. Liam and I got back together when I was in London, and we've been together ever since. He's been here visiting me for the last few weeks. He was going to leave this morning, but he got sick. He's having an emergency appendectomy now, and I think he's already developed peritonitis."

Her father sank heavily onto the nearest chair, as if his knees simply wouldn't hold up to this shock.

She drew a ragged breath, figuring that was about as much as he could handle hearing just yet. "I was going to tell you all that he and I were together again, but then Mother had the stroke and she was so sick, and then the demands of med school were so overwhelming and I…well, I just couldn't find the courage. It was stupid, I know, and there are more things I need to tell you, but…"

Her breath caught on a sob. "I've made such a mess of everything. And now Liam's in surgery and I don't know how he's doing. He looked so very sick when I brought him in. I'm really scared, Dad."

Her father looked torn between shock, anger and dismay. "I don't know what to say, Anne. That you've actually been seeing him all this time, and you've never said a word about it… It's just…"

"I know. And I still haven't told you everything—but I will. I've wanted to tell you so many times. I just didn't know how," she finished miserably. "You were so adamantly against Liam—against me being involved with anyone, actually. You were so sure I couldn't handle both a relationship and medical school. And it hasn't been easy, but it's been working—for the most part. He's been nothing but supportive of me, so careful not to interfere with my studies. He and I had a quarrel last night about that very thing."

"Last night? After I called you?"

She nodded miserably. "He thought he should leave before you and Mom found out about us. I was ready to tell you the truth, but he thought it was too stressful a time for me and he wanted to wait until after Step 1. I told him he was just like you—always trying to make my decisions for me, for my own good, and we both got mad. And he was sick the whole time, but I was so wrapped up in my own pride and temper and worry about tests and classes and family issues that I hardly even noticed. What kind of doctor will I be if I'm so self-absorbed that I can't see someone is suffering right in front of me?"

She was crying now, racked with fear and guilt. Her father hesitated a moment, still dealing with his myriad reactions to everything she had just thrown at him. And then he put his own emotions aside and wrapped an arm around her. "You'll be a very good doctor, Anne. No one expects you to be ready to practice during your second year of medical school. And maybe he didn't tell you everything he was feeling?"

"No," she said with a sniffle. "He hardly complained at all. He said his stomach hurt and that he was a little queasy, but that's pretty much all he told me. I thought he just had that stomach virus that's been going around so much lately."

"Which is exactly what my first reaction would have been if that was all I was told. Was he running a fever? Did he complain of pain in his right side?"

"No. When I got home from class today, he was lying on his side with his knees drawn up. He was running a high fever then, and complaining of nausea and pain. I finally considered what he might have and I did the McBurney pressure test. He had severe rebound pain, which is when I finally realized that he was seriously ill."

"You can't blame yourself. Liam isn't the usual age for appendicitis, and it sounds as if his symptoms did not present in a typical fashion. That's something you'll learn with practice—*typical* is a very relative term when you're dealing with individual patients. They don't all fit on to a neat checklist of symptoms and signs."

"He's been back there for a long time," she said anxiously, twisting her hands in her lap. "What if the appendix ruptured? What if he's developed sepsis?"

Sepsis was an infrequent, but very serious complication from appendicitis. With sepsis, bacteria entered the bloodstream, traveling throughout the body. It could be life threatening.

Her dad covered her hands with his own big, skilled hand. "Then he'll be treated with IV antibiotics. You can probably tell me which ones."

"I don't want to be quizzed right now, Dad," she said with a groan. "I just want to know that Liam's going to be all right."

He nodded and stood. "Wait here. I'll go see what I can find out."

This, she thought, her breath catching on a last sob, was why she had called him. There was no surgeon, no physician she trusted more than her father. Now that he was here, Liam would be all right.

She had to believe that.

She knew there would be much more to be revealed to her family. More explanations, more apologies, more guilt-inducing recriminations from both her parents and probably her grandfather, too. But they would come around, just as she had always known deep inside that they would.

Now if only she would have the chance to bring Liam around, to make him understand how important her family was to her. To convince him that loving them in no way detracted from how much she loved him. That being a part of her family, difficult though they could be, wasn't such a terrible thing.

The question was—did Liam love her enough to accept the whole package? Her family, her career, her strengths and her flaws? Or would it turn out that their whole marriage had been based on a youthful, passion-driven, fantasy-inspired impulse that could not stand up to the day-to-day challenges of the real world?

Praying that she would have the chance to find

out, she drew a deep breath and huddled more deeply into the chair to wait for news.

Liam was so disoriented when he opened his eyes that it took him a little while to figure out where he was. His mind was clouded, probably by the drugs being pumped into his veins through an IV tube, making it hard for him to think coherently.

He remembered bits and pieces—being in the ambulance, bright lights in his eyes, concerned faces leaning over him. He remembered Anne, looking afraid. He remembered her voice, her tone reassuring even though he'd had a hard time focusing on the words. He sort of remembered waking up in recovery, then drifting out again. Had he dreamed that Anne's father had hovered above him at one point? And then Anne, again. Looking increasingly tired and strained.

He had wanted to tell her to get some rest, but he simply hadn't had the energy. He'd slept, waking only in brief, fuzzy snatches, and she had always been there. How much time had passed? Had she slept? Was she missing classes or exams because of him? He didn't want that.

He should have gone back to New York, he thought, closing his eyes on a wave of self-recrimination. He shouldn't have caused even more trouble for Anne. Even though he knew it was unreasonable, he felt almost foolish for having gotten ill at such an inconvenient time. He was oddly chagrined at being so weak and vulnerable at a time when he needed to be strong for Anne.

He forced his eyelids open again, blinking a couple of times to bring the room into focus. He sensed suddenly that he wasn't alone, and he turned his head, expecting to find Anne sitting watch over him.

When he saw who sat there, he wondered for a moment if the meds were making him hallucinate.

"So you're awake," Henry Easton, Jr., said unnecessarily.

"I— Yeah." His voice sounded rusty, as if it

had been days rather than hours since he'd last used it. "Why are you here?"

"Anne wouldn't agree to get any rest until someone agreed to sit with you. Since she was almost asleep on her feet, I told her I'd take babysitting duty for a few hours."

"She, uh—told you?"

"That you're my son-in-law? Yes, she told me. Eventually."

Liam tried to read Easton's expression, finding it very difficult to do so. "You're okay with that?"

"Let's just say you and I have some talking to do yet. But I'll wait until you aren't lying flat on your back."

Liam shifted on the bed, then grimaced when his body rebelled. "I'd appreciate that."

"How are you feeling?"

Liam's succinct response made the older man chuckle. "Has anyone talked to you about your condition?"

"I think so. It's sort of fuzzy. They took out my appendix, right?"

Easton nodded. "You've been out of surgery for about fourteen hours. You developed peritonitis. Almost waited too late to get treatment. You were pretty sick. The antibiotics seem to be working, though, so you'll be back on your feet in a few days. Be a few weeks before you're completely back to normal, though. Hope you weren't scheduled to climb any mountains or wrestle any crocodiles during the next couple of weeks."

"I don't wrestle crocodiles," Liam murmured, wondering if the man had ever actually seen his show.

"Mmm. Bet right now you feel like you took one on, huh?"

"And lost," Liam agreed with a sigh.

"Go back to sleep, if you want. I wouldn't harm a defenseless man."

Maybe that quip was supposed to be reassuring. Liam gave his father-in-law one wary look before letting his heavy lids fall.

"I love her, you know," he muttered as the

drugs and pain drew him toward unconsciousness.

"So do I. Why else would I be sitting here now?"

He would think about that later, Liam decided, letting the darkness take him.

His head felt a little clearer when he woke again. He still hurt, still felt as though he'd been bulldozed, but he knew immediately where he was and why when he opened his eyes.

A male nurse smiled at him as he made notes of the numbers displayed on the vital-signs monitor beside the bed. "Hi, there. I'm Steve. How do you feel?"

"I've been better."

"Are you in pain? On a scale of one to ten, how would you rate your pain level?"

Liam wasn't sure how one went about rating pain, but he made an attempt. "Four. Maybe five," he added with a wince when he tried cautiously to shift into a more comfortable position.

"Okay. I'm putting something in your IV that should make you more comfortable. Let someone know if that isn't enough, all right? We don't want you lying here in pain."

"Thanks, Steve." When the nurse left to tend his other patients, Liam turned his head to look at the chair across the room, wondering if he would find Henry Easton still sitting there, hoping he would see Anne instead.

The chair was empty.

He was okay with that, he assured himself. Easton probably had to work. Anne had classes. He didn't really know anyone else in the area. He didn't need someone sitting with him every minute, anyway. He'd only had major, life-threatening surgery. If he needed anything, all he had to do was push a button and someone on the hospital staff would rush to his side. Probably.

His bout of self-pity was short-lived. Anne entered the room, carrying a lidded, disposable cup that might have held coffee. She smiled when she saw him looking at her, her gaze intently searching his face. "You're awake."

Why did everyone seem to feel the need to announce that to him? "Yes."

"How do you feel?"

He kept his reply rather generic for Anne. "I'm okay."

He glanced at the clock on the wall facing him. Two o'clock—and if he had his days straight, it was Friday afternoon. "Shouldn't you be in class?"

"I skipped classes today. Haley's taking notes for me. I've been sitting in here for the past few hours, since I relieved Dad. He said you'd been awake for a little while this morning."

"Yeah. I was…surprised to see him here."

Setting her coffee on the nightstand beside the bed, Anne stood gazing down at him, her expression hard to read. "I'm sure you were. I didn't think you'd wake up while I was resting, but I wanted someone to be here if you did. Just to reassure you that you'd be okay."

And she'd thought her father would be the one to offer that reassurance? Okay.

"Did you get any sleep?" he asked.

She shrugged, the purplish hollows beneath her eyes giving the real answer before she prevaricated, "Some. I napped in one of the recliners in the waiting room."

So she'd sat with him all night after his surgery. He shook his head against the pillow. "You should have gone home to bed. And you shouldn't have missed classes for me. I'm getting good care here. You should go on now and find your study group. You have to prepare for the next test. Maybe you can stop back in for a little while this evening. I'll be fine until then."

Her eyes narrowed. "I'm the one who decides what I 'should' and 'shouldn't' do, Liam. It's taken me a while to get to that point, but from now on, I don't need anyone making decisions for me. That includes my dad—and you."

He was a bit taken aback by her irritated response. "Uh—sure. Sorry."

Her eyebrows rose in response to his aggrieved tone. "Were you expecting me to cut you some slack because you're lying in a hospital bed?"

"Of course not," he lied. "I was only trying to—"

"Trying to look out for me," she cut in to finish for him. "Just like my family has always done. 'Don't get involved with anyone too early, Anne.' 'Don't let anyone interfere with your studies, Anne.' 'Don't let yourself get distracted from your education, Anne.' 'Don't miss your classes or get behind in your work or fail to do your best on a test or take your eyes from the ultimate goal of surgery, Anne.'"

She leaned over the bed, her hands clenched on the metal railing, her gaze locked with his. "Well, let me tell you, Liam—just as I've already told my dad. All that advice and helpful guidance hasn't been working so well. Because I've tried to please everyone and do everything everyone told me 'for my own good,' I broke up with the man I loved in college. I've worried myself sick through medical school for fear of letting my family down. I made the mistake of secretly getting married and then going to great lengths to keep that secret. And I let myself get so wrapped up in the pressure everyone was putting on me that I didn't even see that my own husband was getting very ill right in front of my miserable and self-absorbed eyes!"

"You couldn't have known—"

"I should have known," she insisted. "I was more concerned about test scores and class ranking than I was about your illness. What kind of doctor does that make me?"

"You're going to be a great doctor. You just have to get through the training, which is so damned hard that no one could possibly blame you for being overwhelmed by it."

She didn't look at all convinced, but he moved on, addressing something else she had said that was bothering him. "You said you 'made the mistake' of secretly marrying."

She lifted her chin a little. "Yes. That's what I said."

He wondered grimly how he would rate the pain he felt now. There wasn't a scale that went high enough to describe the ache in his heart after hearing Anne declare their marriage a mistake. "Does that mean you want a divorce?"

Anne gave a long, deep sigh. "You are such an idiot, Liam McCright."

That was certainly not an answer to the question he had asked. But he felt himself relax somewhat in response to the gentle insult.

She could call him anything she wanted, as long as she didn't change her mind about being married to him, he thought wistfully.

Watching as Liam seemed to draw back into the bed, his face almost as white as the crisp hospital sheets, Anne felt a moment of regret that she hadn't waited to have this conversation later, when he'd had a little more time for recovery. But she was still so angry with herself—and maybe with him, as well—that he had almost died because of their lack of communication, she couldn't wait any longer.

Concerned with his pallor, she placed a gentle hand on his shoulder. "Do you need anything? Are you in pain?"

"I'm already having trouble thinking clearly. I'm okay for now."

"Maybe we should talk about this later," she said, but he shook his head.

"Now you're the one saying what *I* should do for my own good," he muttered.

She had to smile a little at that. "I guess I am. Sorry."

His eyes were dark as they searched her face. "You, uh, you said our marriage was a mistake. Maybe you could elaborate on that a little?"

"I said the way we married was a mistake," she corrected him. "The secret elopement. We— I should have had the courage to take those vows openly, whether anyone else approved or not. I should have told my parents from the beginning that I was seeing you, and that I would continue to do so without their permission. And, we should have spent more time talking and less time playing before we took the step of getting married. We were so intoxicated with the freedom and privacy that we had in

London that we let ourselves forget about the real-world issues that would confront us later. Like our busy schedules. And my family."

"I never meant to try to take you away from your family."

"I think you did see it as a choice between you and them," she replied quietly. "Maybe not consciously. But maybe—well, maybe you needed to believe that I would always put you first. I haven't studied much psychiatry yet, but it isn't hard to imagine you'd have abandonment issues, considering your childhood. The way your father left you, and then your mother died when you were still so young."

He flinched, but she continued without letting him respond, "I understood why your own family background would make it hard for you to understand why I remained close to mine, despite my efforts to be independent from them. I just didn't fully realize you would need to be reassured occasionally that I would never let them keep me away from you. Until we talked with Haley last week, I didn't even realize you blamed them solely for our breakup in college, despite the quarrels you and I had back then that had little to do with them."

A hint of color touched his pale cheeks now. He looked almost sheepish when he muttered, "I'm not a child. I don't need constant reassurance that you aren't going to leave me."

She supposed his stinging male ego made him say that, but she knew it wasn't entirely true. Maybe he didn't need constant reassurance—but he needed to hear it occasionally. Just as she needed to hear from him that their marriage meant more to him than his career or his celebrity or his resistance to becoming part of her family.

His eyelids were beginning to grow heavy, as if he were fighting to stay alert for this ill-timed conversation. "Annie?"

She leaned closer. "Yes?"

"You were right, you know. I'm not all that brave. I've been afraid of a lot of things. I was afraid your parents—or someone else—would take you away from me. I was afraid of trying to fit into your overachieving and overinvolved family. I was afraid of finishing the book and having no other excuse to stay with you—and afraid it will bomb once it's published. And I was so damned afraid that if I left this time, we'd have used up all our chances to make this work out between us."

She didn't know how much of that confession had been fueled by the meds dripping through his IV tube, but there was no mistaking the sincerity of his words.

She laid her hand against his face, speaking very clearly. "I love you, Liam. I always have. I always will."

He reached out to take her hand, and though his grip was still weak enough to melt her heart, his voice was steady. "I love you, too. And I don't care if the whole world knows it."

"That's good," she said, blinking back a mist of tears. "I was told a reporter called the hospital this morning to find out if you're really a patient here. I don't know how the news got out, but it seems that it has. The hospital staff will keep your case confidential, but some tidbits will probably leak out, anyway."

He looked unfazed by that revelation. "I'll call my agent and my publicist later. They'll handle it."

"Whatever you think best."

"Annie—" His words were beginning to slur a little, and his eyelids looked heavier.

"Get some rest, Liam. We can talk more later. We have plenty of time." They would make the time, she promised herself. Whatever it took.

He closed his eyes, then pushed them open again to ask, "Annie—if we weren't already married, and I asked you again now...?"

She smiled, knowing the medications were making him a little loopy, but answering the fanciful question, anyway. "I would say yes, Liam. Always. Forever."

It seemed to satisfy him. Still holding her hand, he closed his eyes. "Me, too. Love you."

She leaned over to brush a tender kiss across his forehead. "I love you, too, Liam."

From this point on, she didn't care if the whole world knew.

Epilogue

Even though the sun was beginning to set, it was still quite warm on this early July Arkansas evening. A sizable crowd had gathered on the sprawling back lawn of Henry and Deloris Easton's home for their long-established Independence Day barbecue. Because of Deloris's health, they'd had to cancel the event for the past two years, but she'd felt well enough this year to insist on reviving the tradition.

Reassuring herself occasionally that her mother was holding up well to the demands of hostessing, Anne mingled with the guests and quietly handled most of the supervision of the catering and festivities. The lawn was attractively crowded with red, white and blue decorated tables and party lights. Discreetly placed fans kept air circulating among the guests, who were heartily enjoying the abundant food offerings. A Dixieland band played on a small, portable stage in one corner, adding to the festive atmosphere, but not so loud to interfere with conversation. All in all, she deemed the event a great success.

She glanced at a table where her study group friends sat eating and laughing. Her mother had insisted Anne invite those friends who had been so supportive in helping Anne survive the past two years of school, and they had all accepted. Connor was accompanied by his wife, Mia, and their daughter, Alexis. Haley had brought her friend Kris. James and Ron had come stag. Ron was actually being civil to Haley's date, though Anne still had her suspicions about Ron's feelings for Haley.

Things would change with the coming school

year, Anne thought a bit sadly. After spending four semesters in the same classes, the group would be split up for rotations. Now that they had all taken Step 1, they wouldn't need to study as a group. They hadn't received their test results yet, but they were all cautiously optimistic that they had passed. The upcoming demands on their time would make it hard for them to get together very often on a social basis, though they had all promised solemnly that they would not let their friendship end with the change in their schedules. She hoped very much that it would prove to be true.

"Your friends seem to be having a good time," Anne's mother commented when their paths crossed at the drinks table. "Go join them. Everything's going smoothly here."

"I will," Anne agreed. "I was just getting a glass of lemonade."

Leaning only lightly on her cane, her mom smiled at her. "Thank you so much for all your help today, sweetheart. I don't know how I would have gotten everything done without you. I'm so glad we decided to have the party. I'm having a wonderful time."

Anne leaned over to brush a quick kiss against her mom's soft cheek. "It's a great party, Mother."

Looking over Anne's shoulder, her mom smiled more brightly. "I think it's about to get better for you. Look who's joined us."

Turning, Anne caught her breath in surprised pleasure. "Liam!" she called out, waving to get her husband's attention as he entered the gate to the back lawn.

He greeted her with a hug that brought her feet off the ground, and a kiss that promised much more to come when they were alone. Grinning, he set her back down.

She laughed happily and rested a hand on his chest. "I thought you were going to be tied up until next week in meetings in New York."

"We wrapped up early. I didn't want to miss watching the fireworks with you."

Hugging him again, she said, "I'm so glad you're here."

"So am I." He moved away from her only far enough to greet her mother with a peck on the cheek. Anne noted that he was getting less awkward with her mother as they'd had time to adjust to each other. He and her brother got along quite well, too.

As for her father and grandfather—well, they were coming around, she thought with a wry smile. The fireworks she had expected in response to her marriage announcement had come after everyone was certain that Liam would recover fully from his emergency appendectomy. There had been recriminations and hurt feelings all around, but her family was too tightly knit to allow their disapproval to split them apart. They'd made certain that Anne was able to finish her second year and take her big exam with the support of her family to bolster her.

Her father and grandfather still took great pleasure in referring to her husband as "that McCright boy," and she couldn't say they were exactly enthusiastic yet about her springing a surprise marriage on them, but they were all polite enough when the family gathered. Liam had already charmed his way into his mother-in-law's good graces, and he was making headway with the men. He made the effort for Anne's sake, and she would always be thankful to him for that, especially knowing that he would have been content to avoid her family altogether.

Liam seemed to have accepted in resignation that Anne's family was now a permanent and prominent part of his life, too. She hoped there would come a day when he'd be grateful for that, but maybe that was asking a little too much.

He had been spending as much time as he could with Anne since he'd been released from the hospital three days after his surgery. His job would always demand a great deal of travel, but his home base would be with her from now on. They were both content with that arrangement for the present. Perhaps in the future, they had agreed, he would concentrate more on writing and producing so he wouldn't have to be gone quite so much, but they would concentrate on that later.

Because he loved her, he was making the best of the situation.

"You're looking well, Deloris," he said, using Anne's mother's first name, as Deloris had requested. "Looks like a great party, too."

"It's going very well," she agreed, "thanks to Anne's help."

It had taken her mom a bit to recover from the shock of learning about Anne's marriage, and from the disappointment that there hadn't been a big, elaborate wedding to plan. She made no secret that she didn't entirely approve of the risks Liam sometimes took in pursuit of a story, but she seemed impressed that he would soon be a published author.

"Alice," she called out, motioning toward a woman passing nearby. "You haven't had a chance to meet my son-in-law yet, have you? This is Liam McCright. He's on TV, you know."

Anne and Liam exchanged a laughing glance before he courteously greeted her mother's friend. Anne stood nearby while he heaped a plate with barbecue and side dishes. Then they joined her study group, who greeted Liam warmly among them, all of them having met him prior to this gathering.

Surrounded by her family and close friends, Anne realized that she had never been happier. She still had a long way to go in her medical training, lots more hard work, grueling exams and exhausting pressure, but she felt more ready now to face those challenges. She would have a fulfilling career, and she would be married to the man she'd loved from the moment she'd met him.

She couldn't ask for anything more.

* * * * *